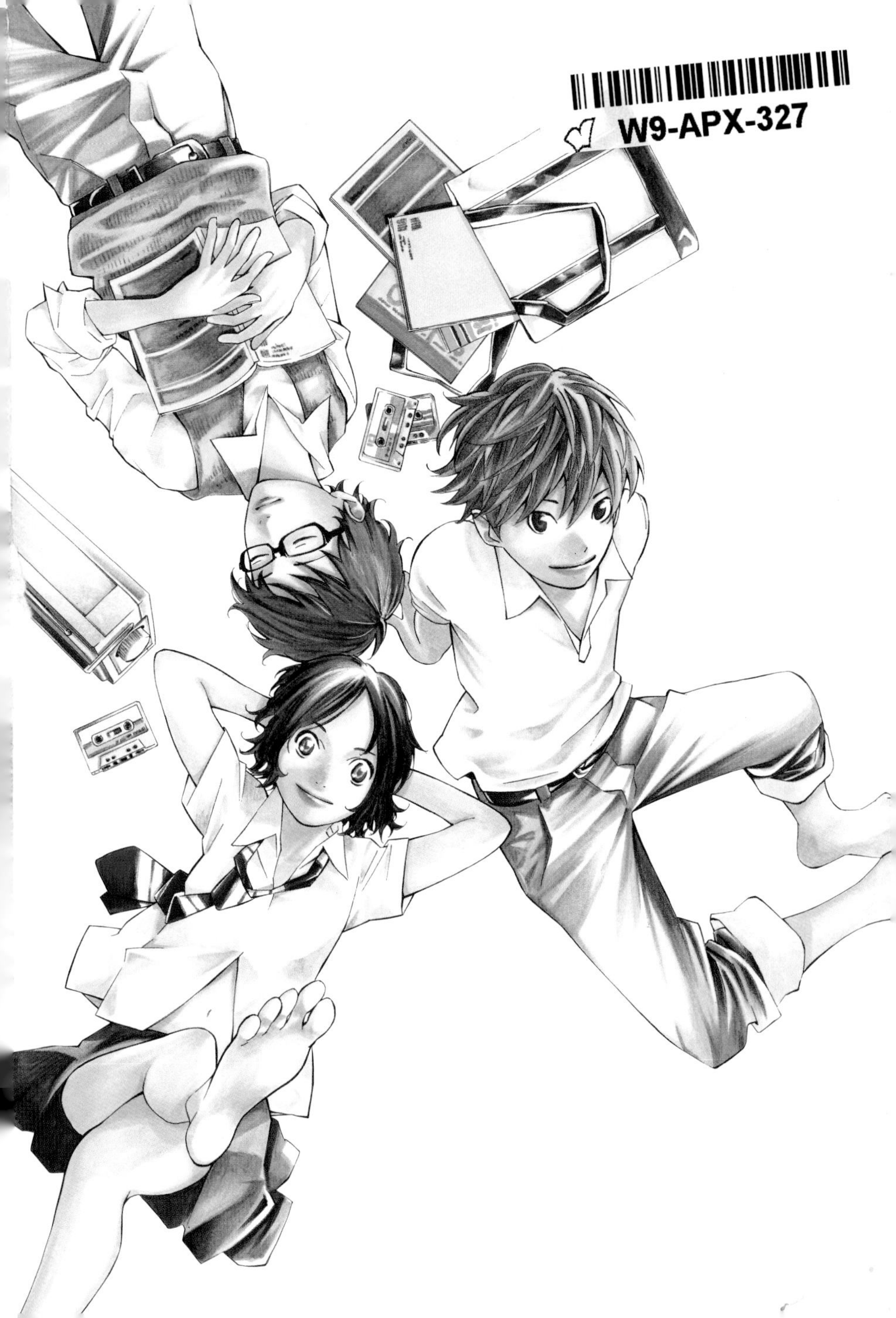

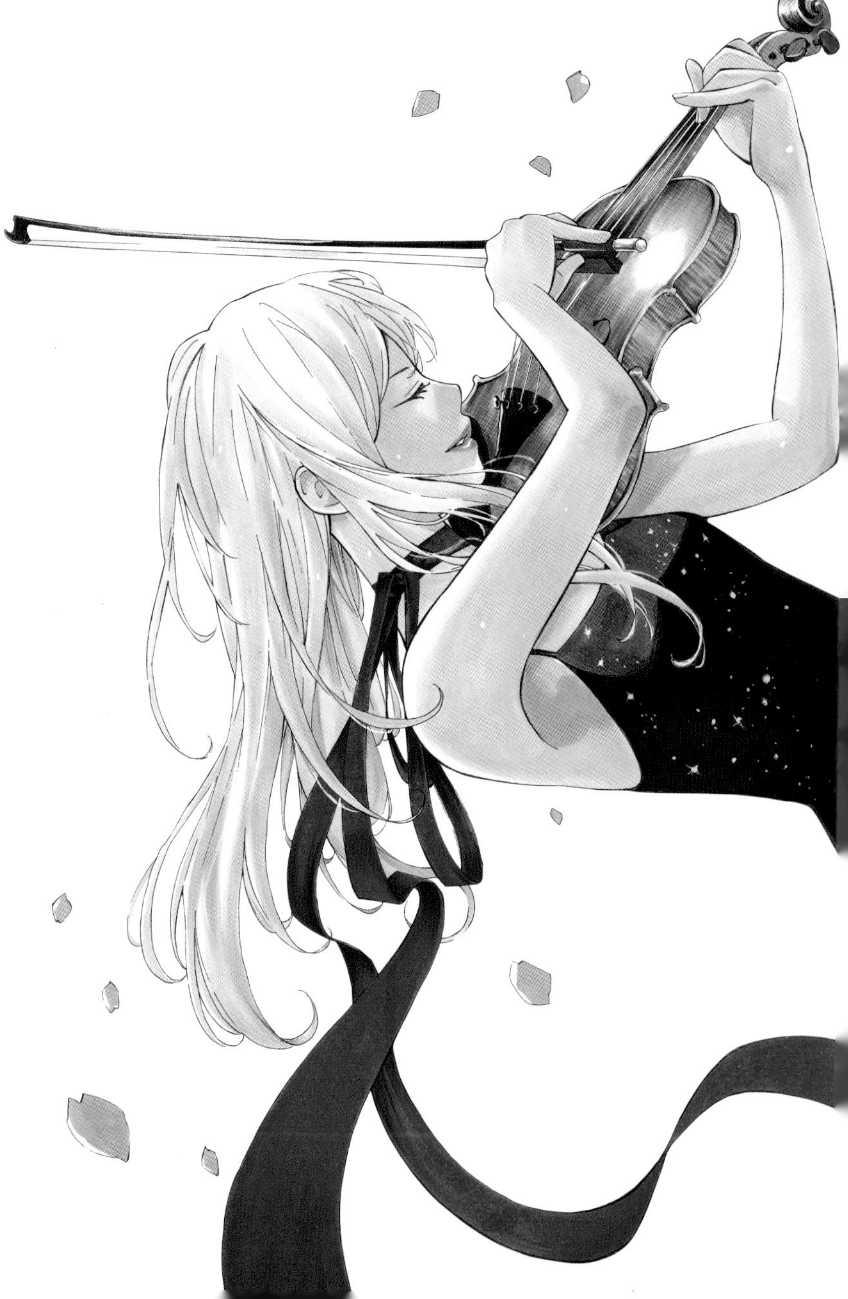

Your Lie in April
A Six-Person Etude

Stories by Yui Tokiumi
Created by Naoshi Arakawa

Translated by Greg Gencarello

Your Lie in April
A Six-Person Etude

© 2014 Yui Tokiumi / Naoshi Arakawa. All rights reserved.
First published in Japan in 2014 by Kodansha, Ltd., Tokyo.
Publication rights for this English edition arranged
through Kodansha Ltd., Tokyo.
English language version produced by Vertical, Inc.

Art by Naoshi Arakawa.

Translated and edited comic pages provided by Kodansha Comics
Translation: Alethea and Athena Nibley
Editor: Paul Starr

Published by Vertical, Inc., New York, 2017

Originally published in Japanese as *Shousetu Shigatu wa
Kimi no Uso Rokunin no Echuudo.*

ISBN 978-1-945054-26-6

Manufactured in the United States of America

First Edition

Vertical, Inc.
451 Park Avenue South, 7th Floor
New York, NY 10016
www.vertical-inc.com

CONTENTS

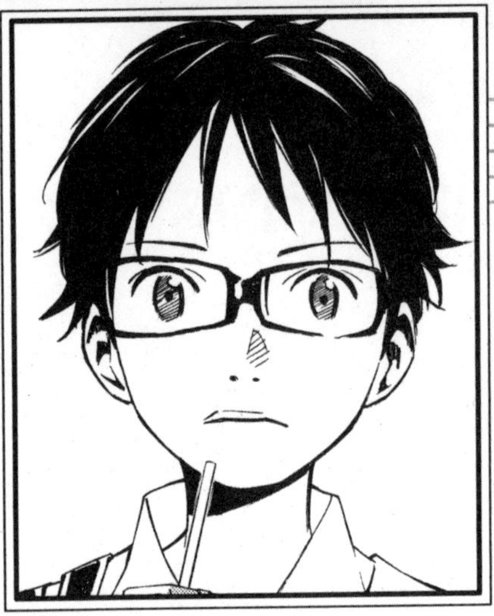

〚Kosei Arima〛

He's taken the top spot at countless music competitions since he was little. He's a genius pianist—or he used to be.

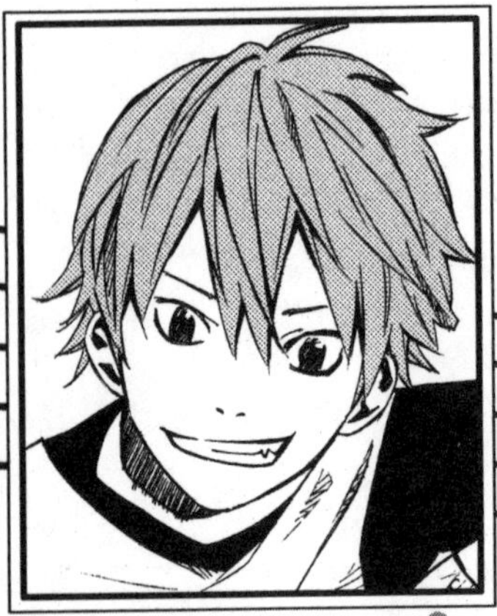

〚Ryota Watari〛

Captain of the soccer club. Friends with Kosei and Tsubaki since they were little. A real hit with the girls.

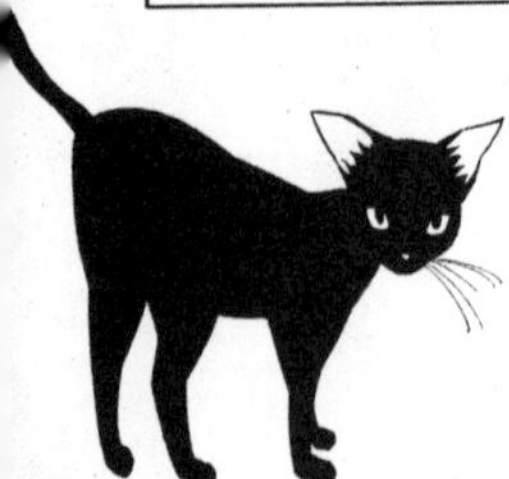

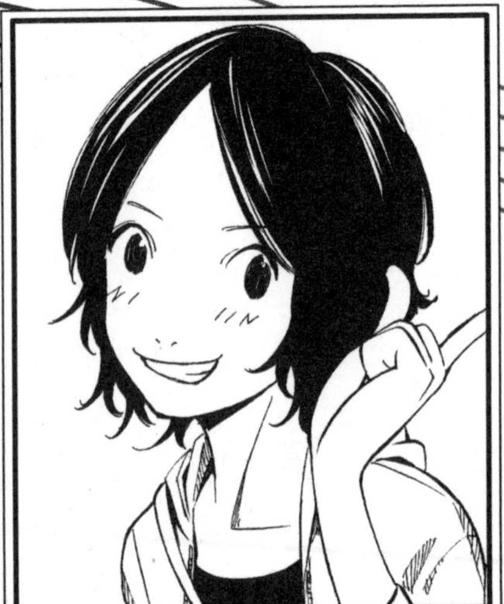

〚Tsubaki Sawabe〛

Kosei's childhood friend, living next door. The big hitter in the softball club.

CHARACTERS

〖 Kaori Miyazono 〗

A violinist with a strong personality all her own. When she suddenly enters the picture one spring, fourteen-year-old Kosei's life begins to change.

〖 Takeshi Aiza 〗

A pianist. After he meets Kosei and Emi when he's eight, they become his lifelong rivals.

〖 Emi Igawa 〗

Moved by Kosei's piano when she's five years old, she resolves to become a pianist.

Prologue 〚 ♪ You're a Wimp 〛 Kaori Miyazono

It's summer break, and our middle school is empty, except for us.

The windows in the music room are wide open, and I can see huge columns of clouds far off in the distance.

From the grove of dark green trees poking out over the rooftops of the residential area, I can hear the cicadas buzzing nonstop.

Since the air conditioner in the room doesn't work, the fan is on, shaking its head. Feeling its warm air wash over me, I place my violin on my left shoulder, ready my bow, and tap a string.

The score that I've spread out on my music stand is "Love's Sorrow" by Fritz Kreisler.

Mi-laa-mii-mii, mi-fa-mi-re-mi-faa...

Sool-ree-ree, re-mi-re-do-re-mii...

The vaguely sad, nostalgic melody cries from my violin.

7

As you sit facing your grand piano, trying to keep up with my melody, you tap out the same notes in one octave with your left hand, and then play a chord twice with your right. This makes a three-beat rhythm.

Dum, dah, dah. Dum, dah, dah.

Yes, that's it!

Wanting the melody to really be pleasant, I put my heart into it, filling the room with my violin's melody...

Hmmm...the tempo's just off somehow.

My violin and your piano are doing their own things.

"Okay, one more time! From the beginning. Let's pick up the tempo a little at the start, and then be careful not to go overboard with the ritardando. Dum, da, da, dum, da, da, like that."

I say this to you, and then ready my bow in my right hand again. When the bow touches the strings, the tone they make echoes through my whole body. Then your piano starts.

But we just can't sync up, no matter what we do.

We start to lose our tempo bit by bit.

You rush to catch the next note, and I draw out the lovely one I'm playing. Our sounds should be matched perfectly, but instead they're out of step, as if our hearts were growing further and further apart.

I stop playing.

"This isn't working," I say. "Let's take it from the top."

Still facing the piano, you nod without saying a word.

You lost the person who mattered to you the most, and you lost the sound you created together, too.

You're weak. You're a wimp.

Why are you turning your back on the memories you two

had?

Why've you closed your heart to that sound?

But...I want you to know, you're not really a wimp. I want everyone to know that, but you most of all.

"What's going on? You're off by a quarter beat. Let's do it again, from the start!"

Now I'm all revved up and it's you who can't catch up with me. Your piano's lagging behind my violin, getting dragged along and practically stumbling.

"C'mon, let's go!"

"Ahh, let's do it over."

"No, no! Once more, from the key change!"

"How come it keeps falling apart right there? All right, one more time."

We can't even make it to the end of a three-and-a-half-minute song. We start over again and again. By the end, we're drenched in sweat.

"You aren't even trying to be in sync with me, are you?"

I bring the violin down from my shoulder, sulking a bit. You smile weakly at me, unsure what to do.

"Your playing is so free. I'm barely able to keep up."

"Huh? You're saying it's my fault?"

"No, no, I'm just saying that's how you always are. Could you maybe give me a cue? Like, tell me when you're gonna hold the note longer than what's on the sheet?"

"I'm not holding the notes, I'm just letting the sound

GRIP

NOTE: All manga inserts are printed in their original format.
Start reading at the top right.

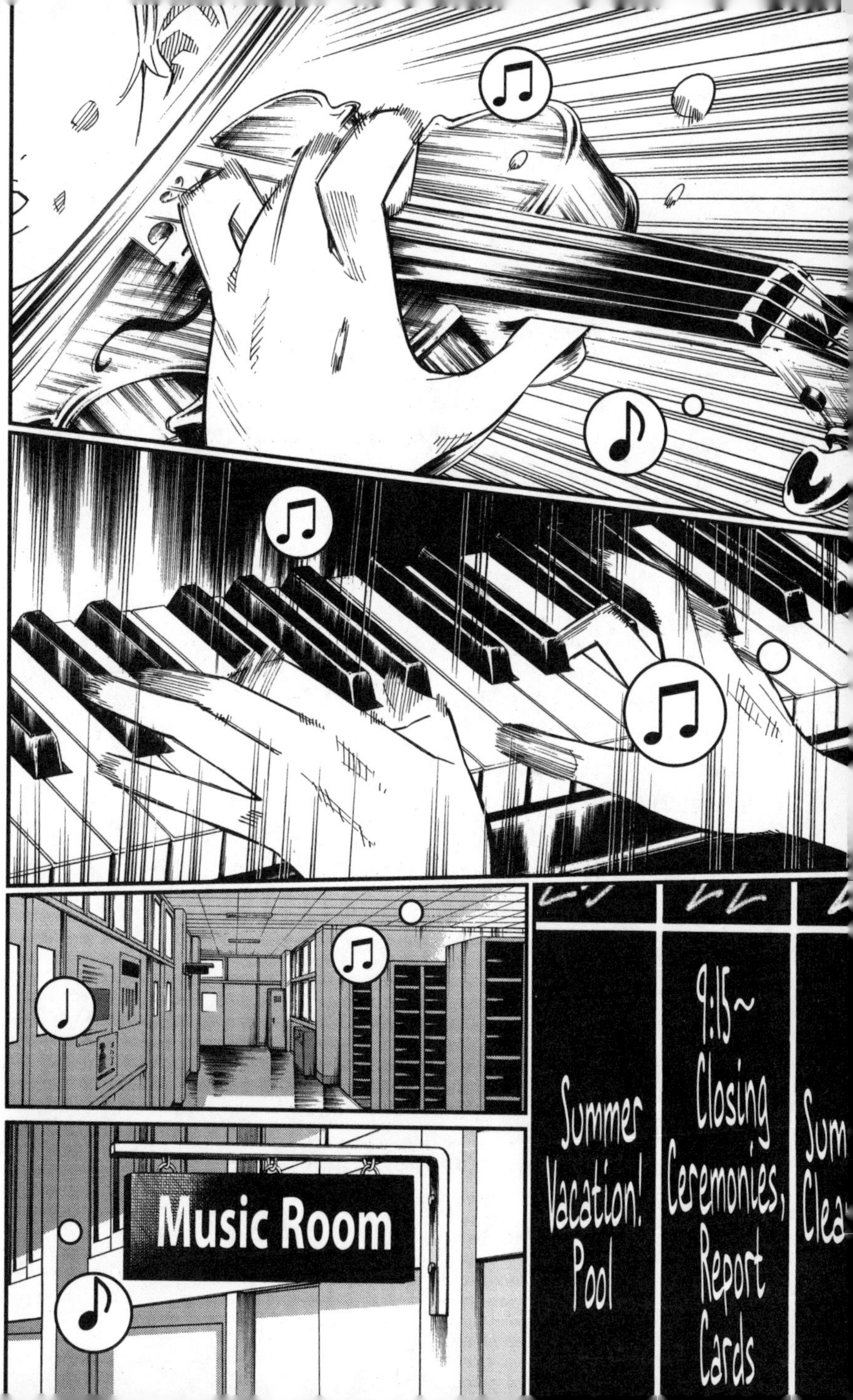
Music Room
Summer Vacation! Pool
9:15~ Closing Ceremonies, Report Cards

resonate 'cause it feels good. If you wait for me to give you a cue, you'll be way too late. Watch me carefully. Really look at me. Then you'll know!"

"Aw, how can I..."

"What do you mean, how can you? Here, I'll show you, like this."

I get closer to you. We're so close that our foreheads are almost touching, and I'm looking into your eyes. I can see my reflection in them, behind the lenses of your nerdy, black-rimmed glasses.

"Your, your face... It's too close."

You flinch, pulling away from me.

"What? I gotta be this close."

"For real?"

"Well, I think so. Anyway, let's try it!"

I stare at your profile, while you study me with a sideways glance. We get ourselves in sync and are just about to play our first notes when...

"Hey guys, what's up?"

"Kaori, Kosei, ice cream time!"

The door in the back of the music room bursts open, and in come Ryota Watari and Tsubaki Sawabe, with a convenience store bag in hand.

Ryota pulls out an ice cream bar and thrusts it towards me, like a mic.

"How're you feeling about your first duet concert, Miss Miyazono?"

"Oh, I feel super honored! I'm so proud that the sponsor asked me to play in this gala concert!"

Seeing me put on this act, Ryota smiles.

"Of course you were chosen, Kaori. With your talent, you're

gonna blossom on the stage, like a rose."

Oh, what a cool guy, Ryota. It's no lie when they say he's the biggest chick magnet in our year...scratch that, in all of Sumiya Middle School.

"Man, watching you play your violin got me wishing I could play piano. To think Kosei here is gonna be standing with you on stage, when it should be me."

"Yeah," you say, "besides the piano I don't have much going for me."

You answer him calmly without shrinking a bit. Then Tsubaki holds out an ice cream bar to you.

"It's gonna melt. You want the milk-flavored one, right, Kosei?"

Taking it from her, you get up and walk away from the piano.

"Thanks, Tsubaki."

We all sit down on the platform in the music room side by side—Ryota, then me, then you a little farther away, and finally Tsubaki—and eat our ice creams.

"So, you like the milk-flavored one, huh?" I say to you as you sit on my left.

"Yep." You nod, your eyes locked on your ice cream bar to tear the package open.

"I didn't know that. I had you as a chocolate kind of guy, for some reason."

"Me? Why would that be?"

"Well, that's why I said *for some reason.*"

I didn't know the milk-flavored one was your favorite, but Tsubaki knew. You two have been friends for ages, after all.

"Go ahead and eat it, before it melts," I urge. You've been

waiting for me, without having a taste.

"Okay," you reply curtly, and without missing a beat, start munching rhythmically on your ice cream bar.

"*I* like chocolate," Tsubaki says, pulling out another bar from the bag.

"Me too, me too," I say, choosing a chocolate-flavored one for myself.

"Right? Who doesn't?"

We nod at each other.

"I wonder why Kosei always goes for the milk ones," Tsubaki mutters. "From way back."

I look at you out of the corner of my eyes.

"Don't you wanna try different kinds? Tsubaki took the trouble to buy all these flavors...well, only three kinds, but still."

"Well, Tsubaki *did* give it to me."

"Oh, so you're gonna blame someone else?"

"No, either way I'd pick the milk one. I like what I like," you say, brushing it off.

You really do like doing things your way. You're so stubborn.

Sure, you won't ever defy other people, but in your heart of hearts, you stick to your opinion and don't give an inch.

You're so weak. You never set yourself up against somebody else.

But even though you look like you're weak, deep down you're strong. Always holding onto your beliefs, no matter what. Maybe you don't realize it yourself, but really, you are strong. I believe you are.

"So you like the chocolate one, right, Kaori? Got it. I'm a chocolate kinda guy too," Ryota says, trying to smooth over this awkward conversation. "Hang on...ah, all we've got left is the soda-flavored one! Well, I *do* like that one too."

"But Ryota, you don't really care," Tsubaki says. "That one time when Keiko said she liked the milk flavor, you said, 'Me too.'"

"That's because it would've been rude to the people making the ice cream if I said I didn't like one of the flavors."

Ryota is laughing, innocently. He's so cool, and so thoughtful, and so kind. And Tsubaki is such a good person, too. I feel happy to be so blessed with good friends.

"So, about the concert, is it okay if we come to hear you play?" Ryota asks with a pleasant smile, gazing at me.

His smile is comforting. I get why so many people take a liking to him. *I* like him. And Tsubaki does, too.

"Sure you can. Both of you should come."

"I asked you before if gala concerts were like exhibition games in sports, and you said 'Bingo,' didn't you, Kaori?"

"You mean like a figure-skating exhibition?" asks Tsubaki. "Like an extra freebie?"

Since she's asking, I explain.

"Yeah. You can play however you want, since you're not stressing over being scored anymore. Some people even pick songs that are harder to play than the ones they're assigned for the competition, because they don't have to worry about messing up. It's your golden chance to shine, to really express yourself as you are. It really makes the stage sparkle!"

At a competition, you have to follow what's written on the music sheet, and you're judged on how accurately you perform, like a machine. No matter how moved the audience is by your personal style, ignoring the composer's directions and playing how you want will hurt your score.

As for me, I'm all about my own style.

Which means my competition record had nothing to do with me being in the concert. I only barely made the cut thanks to a recommendation quota.

But that's okay. It's my own sound that I want to give to others, that I want to let ring. I want it to linger in people's hearts after they hear it.

This summer, if the two of us come together, I can do that.

I want to play my heart out. And then I want to laugh with you.

♯ 1 ⟦ ♪ Kosei's My Hero ⟧ Takeshi Aiza

It's June. I'm in the outskirts of the western part of Tokyo, in a township that's too big to be called a ward but just barely a city. It's a residential area with lots of greenery, where the houses have tiny gardens with lawns, and everyone's got a luxury car sitting in the garage.

I'm inside one of those houses right now.

"Takeshi, you going to do this or what?"

That's my teacher, Akira Takayanagi. He sounds exasperated, like he's about given up. Then he plops down into the sofa behind the piano, folding his hands behind his head, and gives a loud sigh.

"What, think you can just take it easy, like you'll get away with phoning it in at practice?"

Damn...guess I'm busted, I mutter in my head as I sit facing the piano.

Cut me a break, man. After school, we went head-to-head

against Class One—I'm in Class Two, the next room over, and we're all in fourth grade—in a soccer game, where our pride was on the line. Okay, well, they'd egged us on to play them, and since I'm the fastest runner in my class, the team would've lost without me, you know?

I had to spend two hours after school every day this week practicing for the game. I was wiped, and on my best day I could play piano for two hours. I was basically good for about one hour, and besides, it's no fun playing basic etudes where you just practice your finger movements. Well, for set pieces I guess I'd do it.

"Do you even really want to catch up with Kosei Arima, and become better than him?"

"...Yeah."

Kosei's my hero. He's awesome. He's got the strength to never lose.

He plays his set-piece music perfectly. His performances are flawlessly accurate, and he has the guts not to choke under pressure.

"If so, there's only one answer. There's too big a gap between how much you practice. Once you put in as much practice as he does, go ahead and talk a big game about catching up to him, and whatnot."

"How much time are we talking?" I ask, pouting my lips as I turn back to look at Mr. Takayanagi.

I practice every day. If I take even one day off, my fingers don't move right for three days.

"Every morning, I suppose he plays for an hour before going to school, and after class he must do another four hours or so. At least one of those hours he's got to be working on his basic etudes. After that, he'll drill the piece into his head. He'll break it up and take it two measures at a time, until they're perfect. When he's done that for all four pairs, he'll go all the way through from one to eight until it's all perfect. Then he'll repeat that...well, probably."

"No way! That's sooooo boring, practicing that much. I like to practice the whole thing start to finish."

"If you do that, you trick yourself into thinking you can play it, and you end up missing the little details. Wasn't it your goal to play perfectly like a machine, with no mistakes or weak spots, and consistently?"

"Well, yeah...but I don't want to practice something so boring."

Mr. Takayanagi stands up and leans down close to my face with a serious look. "If you want to be great, you have to believe in yourself."

Nighttime.

My folks live in a new housing area, not as green or stylish as Mr. Takayanagi's neighborhood. It takes as long as fifteen minutes to get to by bus from the private rail station, plus our place is in an alley off the main street.

When I get home from Mr. Takayanagi's piano lesson, the first thing I do is rush to my room and take out the program from the district preliminary round of the piano competition the other day. I barely made it. Guess who blew way past everyone in the prelim? Kosei Arima, a fourth grader just like me.

Since it was the whole elementary school section, there were fifth and sixth graders competing too, but out of everybody he took the prized top spot. This was my fourth time to play in the same contest as Kosei. He's come in first every time.

The first time I met Kosei was at the same district prelim,

exactly a year ago. It was my first competition.

I didn't really want to be a professional pianist, I just thought I'd give it a try.

About two months before that, I'd just begun third grade. One day, it was my group's turn to clean the music room, when I found a music score still sitting on the closed lid of the grand piano. It was Mozart's "Turkish March," which the music teacher had played in class that day. I flipped through the sheets, and it looked like I could play it, so I did.

My classmates were so impressed...heck, so was the music teacher. I felt great so I played it for Mr. Takayanagi, too. After playing it once I remembered pretty much the whole thing.

"The 'Turkish March'...that's Mozart's Piano Sonata No. 11, 3rd movement. You almost know it by heart after playing just once...and already at such a fast tempo?"

From the pile of papers and music books on the table next to the sofa, Mr. Takayanagi picked out a music book that had a brand-new tag and no bent corners. He opened it to the page with the tag on it and gave it to me.

"Can you play this one?"

"Yeah. You mean like this?"

I made a few mistakes, but it came together somehow on my first try.

"I knew it... Takeshi, I've taught you for almost four years now, and I've often been surprised by how fast you've improved and how good your intuition is. But you're moody and hate practicing and can't apply yourself unless I dangle a carrot in front of you."

Mr. Takayanagi thought to himself for a while.

"All right, then," he muttered at last. "If I promised to buy you a Hero Transformation Belt of your choosing, would you try playing this piece in a competition?"

"A competition? I'd have to practice a lot, right? No thanks."

He got closer to me, full of excitement.

"That's why I'm saying I'll buy the belt. It's precisely the piece I singled out for the piano competition that's being sponsored by the company Neo Musika. Don't you wanna know how much better you can play than the other kids? It's like how everyone knows you're the fastest in your class when you run a sprint race—it's the same with the piano. It's obvious who's got the goods and the talent."

That's how I ended up participating in my first competition a year ago, which is when I met my super-awesome hero.

My hero...Kosei Arima, the one who got called a child prodigy playing one of Mozart's Piano Concertos with an orchestra last month.

In competitions, people usually play from memory, but most of the time they forget little details because they're nervous. The scores have too many directions. It's not just which key you have to tap, it's also the length of the key, how loud or how soft, the tempo, how your fingers move, the Italian words telling you all sorts of vague sensations, like to make it sound like singing, or to play more intensely or relaxed, whether you step on the pedal or not, and...you get the idea.

Especially if you mess up your fingering and play with a different finger than you're supposed to like a klutz, you'll end up touching the wrong key because your finger can't reach the key for the next note, and the length of your notes will end up sounding weird or you'll put in an extra sixteenth rest that's not on the sheet.

Those directions are put there by the composers, but they're for adult players. These are competitions for elementary school kids playing with tiny hands, so of course the performances can't be perfect. The mistouches, noises, and strange silences coming from our fingers not being able to reach mean that we stumble through our performances.

It's not easy for the listeners to get through, either.

But Kosei was different. First, the song he picked was a little tough, and cool too.

It was Beethoven's Piano Sonata No. 17 in D minor, Op. 31/2, 3rd movement—people usually call it "The Tempest." That means a storm. I knew the song.

Kosei played it exactly like a professional pianist you'd hear on a CD, just the way it's written in the sheet music with no mistakes. It was an impressive performance, worthy of a song with an awesome title like "The Tempest."

Whoa...just whoa.

I'd already had my turn near the start of the competition and was in the audience listening to him play. I didn't really care that my ranking wouldn't be so great, and my teacher had said it'd be good for me to hear the other kids' performances. He said I'd see for sure that they all practiced harder than me.

Not that there'd been someone that amazing or anything.

Nobody here's that different from me. Maybe I'll even end up with a way higher score than I thought? I mean, I didn't make any huge mistakes—nothing worse than being a little fast with my tempo.

I'd even started to get bored, but then came the shock.

Whoa! Where'd he come from? He's too good! His playing's matching the score perfectly.

It wasn't just me who thought it was freaky. Almost all the contestants and most of the audience did too.

Well, Kosei's fans and the judges looked like they knew what to expect, but everyone else.

When he finished playing, he got up and bowed to the audience.

The place went totally quiet for a moment. That hadn't happened for any of the other kids.

Then a second later, the crowd broke out into applause. There was a big commotion and people were so impressed they were sighing, and from every direction around me, I could hear people whispering.

"Look at that—any kid who plays with the pros is something else."

"I thought that stuff about playing with a real orchestra was just a way of getting attention, but with talent like this he can be a professional!"

But Kosei didn't look happy at all. He wasn't blushing, and he wasn't giving a polite smile, either. He didn't even try to act all big. Without moving a single hair of his eyebrows, which were lined up with the frame of his nerdy glasses, he hurried off the stage.

He's like some cool gunman from a Western. Like he just had a life-or-death duel with a bad guy and is leaving now with an everyday look on his face. A super-alloy robot with a heart of steel and skills nobody can rival. So strong, so cool!

He was a hero.

Kosei was my hero.

I wanted to be crazy good like that, too. I wanted to be invincible. I wanted to be able to play my sheet music perfectly, with no mistakes, doing exactly what it says on the pages.

Ever since then, Kosei Arima's been my goal.

I check the listings in the program to remind myself of the name of the elementary school Kosei goes to. It's a public school, Hibari Elementary.

It never mattered to me before, but his school is actually in the city bordering mine. And on top of that, his neighborhood is next to mine.

Oh, that's not very far. Wonder if I can bike there?

—If you want to be great, you have to believe in yourself.

"O-kay! Tomorrow I'm gonna find out what Kosei's practice routine is like."

♪

The next day, my classes finish before lunch because we happened to have one of our occasional school events. After lunch and our cleaning chores, I head home.

I ride my bike over to Hibari Elementary where Kosei goes. I know how to get there—first I go straight along a bus route that runs through the residential area near my home, then go over the private railroad, then go a little further through the busy area in front of the station, and finally trace another bus route.

I can see the school right in front of me. I park my bike at a small playground in an apartment complex, tie it to a car stop pole with my wire to lock it, and go toward the school gate.

The street in front of the school gate is lined with rows of zelkova trees. Stealthily, I peer past the gate from behind a big zelkova. Seems like I made it there just before school let out. I spot Kosei in the huge crowd of kids. He's the skinny, bigheaded boy wearing the nerdy black-rimmed glasses. He plods along by himself, his eyes cast down.

Yeah! Found him.

I follow him quietly. On the way, a girl with short hair passes me by and it looks like she invites him to hang out, but he turns her down and goes straight home.

"So, this is the place..."

He says "I'm home" as he goes inside a stylish two-story house. It's got a tiny little garden but is almost touching the house next door, which is pretty common in residential areas. Seriously, they're packed so close.

Since my sister started playing piano a year after I did, my parents had the walls in the piano room soundproofed so we wouldn't bother the neighbors.

Kosei's house is probably the same way. I sit next to the entrance and wait, but I don't hear a piano.

Damn, is he really practicing?

That's when I notice that a middle-aged woman who's walking her dog is standing there and looking at me.

Yikes!

I walk over one block and come back, so she doesn't get the wrong idea. Then I squeeze my body into the gap—where there's some low fencing on each side—between Kosei's house and the neighbor's. "Sawabe," the nameplate on the place next door says.

It's so narrow that a kid's body barely fits through.

Now I can just make out the sound of a piano, which I couldn't from the front of the house. The music room's probably on the other side of the wall. What I hear coming through is a simple melody...do-la-sol-la-fa-la-mi-la, re-ti-la-ti-sol-ti-fa-ti...

It's a basic exercise...Hanon No. 6.

Hanon's a thick piano textbook we use for finger exercises, moving our fingers and building up the muscles in our pinkies and ring fingers, which are usually weak. None of the practice songs in there have any melody or anything, it's just got sixty boring songs with different patterns.

For example, the very first song, Exercise No. 1, has this string of simple notes—do-mi-fa-sol-la-sol-fa-mi—that make up the first measure. After every measure, you skip a key going up for each note, and you do this for two octaves. Then the pattern changes to sol-mi-re-do-ti-do-re-mi, and you skip a key going back down for each note. Repeat this twice, and that's the song. For Exercise No. 2, it's do-mi-la-sol-fa-sol-fa-mi.

It's kind of like vocal practice in a chorus club, where everyone sings "doo-mii-sool-mii-doo" in higher and higher scales. As a rule, your right and left hands make the exact same movements, but they're placed in different positions one octave apart.

And that goes on and on in groups of sixteenth notes.

There's really nothing interesting about it at all.

First you play No. 1 and No. 2 four times, going back and forth and playing them with different rhythms. Next you continue with No. 3, No. 4, and No. 5, cycling through them four times, and then you play a set of No. 6, No. 7, and No. 8 four times. Even just the first section has twenty songs and seven sets.

Kosei plays it like a master, tapping the keyboard as fast as seven times a second. That's the fastest of all the speeds listed in the sheet music. He's scary fast. And with perfect accuracy, without skipping over any notes, and without losing speed, he keeps on tapping his keys.

Creepy...how's he able to keep playing without stumbling or skipping any notes or anything? His concentration's awesome.

With this kind of simple practice stuff, usually what happens is you lose your concentration at some point, or something else pops into your head, and you end up skipping the note you're supposed to play, and the second you skip over a key and slip up, you forget what you were just playing.

Kosei's the man. There's no way I can do that.

And yet...assuming he's playing in order from No. 1, he's played for about an hour without making any mistakes. He's so great, and his notes sound so beautiful and in harmony. But at the same time, I'm kinda getting tired just listening to him— it's like, okay, enough already, I get the idea.

Well, I'm gonna be stubborn. I'll keep listening until he gets to the set piece. Don't wanna waste a chance like this.

I glance at my wristwatch.

Man, it's hot... Right, the rainy season's already here. It's even worse when the sun's out. Ugh, it's so hot, and so humid. I can feel the sweat oozing out of my pores on my back. The soundproofed room must have an air conditioner keeping it nice and cool.

Ti-do-mi-re-do-re-mi-do... That means he's started playing the set from No. 12 to No. 14... Come on, man, isn't it time to stop? Are you really gonna play through all the way to No. 20?

I wait, counting off the songs that are left to play. The sound keeps going on, like a machine is playing, and doesn't even stay in my head anymore—it's just in one ear and out the other.

I can wait just because I know how many songs are left, but otherwise this would be totally unbearable... Hang on, there's no way he's gonna play all sixty...the scale from No. 32, three and then six chords from No. 48, the octave played with one hand...

Unbelievable, the day would come to an end just doing the finger practice.

I really get how intense Kosei's practice is, so I decide that if he starts playing No. 21 I'm just gonna leave.

Thank god, he gets to No. 20 and the Hanon's finally done. Now, he starts playing a real song. The Well-Tempered Clavier No. 1: Prelude and Fugue in C major, by Bach...one of the set pieces for the next competition.

The early part, called the Prelude, is known as an accompaniment to Gounod's "Ave Maria."

When it comes to set pieces for advanced players in piano competitions, most of the time you have to pick from one or two out of the four big genres: there's Baroque, where Bach is usually the go-to choice; Classical, like Haydn, Beethoven, and Mozart; Romantic, where Chopin's a big favorite but once in a while you get maybe Liszt or Brahms; and Modern, which is everything that comes after those.

Nevertheless, it's rare for Modern songs to be chosen. Mostly it's Bach, Beethoven, Mozart, or Chopin, composers whose faded old portraits are hanging on the wall of the music room in any elementary school. You know, like the portraits whose eyes move late at night in those creepy stories or the Seven Classroom Wonders.

Anyway, Kosei starts playing the "Ave Maria piano accompaniment," which many people would probably say they've heard before...but only somebody like me can tell that it's "Ave Maria."

Because he plays just the very first measure of the Prelude—da-da da-da-da da-da-da, da-da da-da-da da-da-da, a phrase made up of eight sounds, twice, and that's it. Then he goes back and starts all over again. Da-da da-da-da da-da-da, da-da da-da-da da-da-da.

Or as we say in musical notes, do-mi sol-do-mi sol-do-mi,

do-mi sol-do-mi sol-do-mi, in C major.

He plays it accurately, with the same length, the same strength, and every sound the same in quality. Da-da da-da-da da-da-da, da-da da-da-da da-da-da. Then again. Da-da da-da-da da-da-da, da-da da-da-da da-da-da.

Seriously? How many times do you play the first measure? It's beautiful...everything is perfect, exactly the same tempo and strength as the sheet says. His finger form is just right—it's not like his right middle finger is too strong, or anything. Tap and release, with all his fingers obeying. No matter how many times he plays, they're all accurate.

Da-da da-da-da da-da-da, da-da da-da-da da-da-da. Da-da da-da-da da-da-da, da-da da-da-da da-da-da.

I'm so lost in the sound I forget to count...but he plays it ten times, maybe.

Finally, he moves on to the second measure, da-da da-da-da da-da-da, da-da da-da-da da-da-da. That's do-re la-re-fa la-re-fa, do-re la-re-fa la-re-fa. This time, I try to count. Yep, ten times.

So he plays ten times for the second measure, too. Then he plays the two measures all at once, da-da da-da-da da-da-da, da-da da-da-da da-da-da, da-da da-da-da da-da-da, da-da da-da-da da-da-da.

And next is the third measure. Da-da da-da-da da-da-da, da-da da-da-da da-da-da. That's ti-re sol-re-fa, sol-re-fa, ti-re sol-re-fa sol-re-fa. Da-da da-da-da da-da-da, da-da da-da-da da-da-da. Da-da da-da-da da-da-da, da-da da-da-da da-da-da. Da-da da-da-da da-da-da, da-da da-da-da da-da-da.

Sometimes the sound doesn't come out perfectly...I think. Those times he repeats more than usual...right? His rule is he goes on to the next one after playing perfectly ten times— maybe?

I'm so excited. I've never heard the sound repeated so accurately.

Awesome, super awesome. He is Kosei, after all.

Then come the fifth and sixth measures, da-da da-da-da da-da-da, da-da da-da-da da-da-da, da-da da-da-da da-da-da, da-da da-da-da da-da-da.

Then the seventh and eighth measures, da-da da-da-da da-da-da, da-da da-da-da da-da-da, da-da da-da-da da-da-da, da-da da-da-da da-da-da.

I'm just like, *Wow.*

These are very simple, with no chords. So they'd sound really boring if they're played poorly.

His piano plays so beautifully. Each sound twinkles. Each sound is alive, and feels so here and real.

He's keeping the same rhythm, so it's not like each one twinkles a different way. But there isn't even one sound that's missing or unclear or bumpy. The notes all shine the same way one after another, every grain of sound comes to life flawlessly. Like pearls rolling out one by one.

Da-da da-da-da da-da-da, da-da da-da-da da-da-da. Da-da da-da da-da-da, da-da da-da-da da-da-da.

This was originally composed as a practice song, too. It's simple, but I feel like I want to hear all the way to the end if I can, unlike those finger exercises before.

As I listen to the music repeating, I start getting this nice, warm feeling. The melody's so beautiful. Bach's such a great composer.

Da-da da-da-da da-da-da, da-da da-da-da da-da-da. Da-da da-da-da da-da-da, da-da da-da-da da-da-da. Da-da da-da-da da-da-da, da-da da-da-da da-da-da. Da-da da-da-da da-da-da, da-da da-da-da da-da-da.

Ah, I'm gonna start falling asleep. No, not 'cause I'm bored—it's just so pleasant that I'm drifting off...and now I'm not. He stumbles and I'm awake again.

He plays it another ten times—da-da da-da-da da-da-da, da-da da-da-da da-da-da—starting over from one phrase earlier.

With all that repeating he did, how long did it take him to play all thirty-five measures of the song?

No way, I can't hold it in anymore, I need to pee!

Damn. Even though part of me wants to stay, I decide to run off.

♪

You know what I realized? What Mr. Takayanagi said is right, period.

I never knew how comforting music can be. That's what I gained.

Here inside a convenience store bathroom, I mutter it over and over. "He was right."

I buy a sports drink with the 150 yen that I've got tucked away in the back pocket of my cargo pants, and gulp the whole thing down in the parking lot. Then I head back to the kids' playground and hop on my bike.

My head is swirling round and round with the thought that he was right, and the piano notes that Kosei kept tapping—da-da da-da-da da-da-da, da-da da-da-da da-da-da, da-da da-da-da da-da-da, da-da da-da-da da-da-da. Even as I start pedaling and head home, the whole time these thoughts stay with me.

Those lovely sounds keep on ringing inside my brain.

Da-da da-da-da da-da-da, da-da da-da-da da-da-da. Da-da da-da-da da-da-da, da-da da-da-da da-da-da.

Those sounds, so perfectly the same, never going away. They keep coming to life, one after another.

Da-da da-da-da da-da-da, da-da da-da-da da-da-da. Da-da da-da-da da-da-da, da-da da-da-da da-da-da.

Does he repeat that kind of practice every day? Day after day, hour after hour, until the sheet music soaks deep down into his core, until he can recreate everything perfectly just like the sheet says?

Making it back to where the streets are familiar, I stop my bike and stare at the palms of my hands.

"It hasn't...soaked in, has it? It feels like the notes are just floating over my palms..."

I rub my hands against my chest and grab my T-shirt.

"The notes will never be part of me. Not at this rate."

I pedal my bike really fast.

I rush into my house. "Homework done?" my mom asks me from the kitchen, but I ignore her. I wash my hands in a hurry and then open the lid of my piano. It's a real grand piano, a recent step up from the old upright we used to have.

I rummage through the colored storage box next to the piano and pull out the same score that Kosei was playing.

I set the score in place and take a seat, get both hands ready over the white keys, and take a deep breath.

I tap them softly.

Da-da, da-da-da da-da-da, da-da, da-da-da, da-da-da. Da-da, da, da-da, da-da-da, da-da, da-da-dadda-da-da. Do-mi, sol-do-mi, sol, do-mi, do-mi, sol-do, mi, sol-do-mi. Do-re, la-re-fa-la, re-fa, do-re, la-re-fa-la-re-fa. Da-da, da-da-da-da-da-da, da-dadda-da-da, da-da-da. Da-da, da-da-da, da-da-da, da, da, da-da-dadda-da-da.

"Ack, I'm getting stuck. My pinkies are weak. No, this is all wrong. Damn, Kosei's really good."

He's my hero, for sure. Nobody can beat him. He's too awesome.

Wonder if I can ever be like that?

"Hey, Teach, you think I can be unbeatable, too? If I really do it right."

I ask Mr. Takayanagi this at my next lesson as soon as I sit down in front of the piano. Mr. Takayanagi's eyes open wide.

"Really do it right, huh? My, my. What's gotten into you?"

"There's no other way to be the best, is there—besides sitting at the piano for hours and hours, and playing the same notes so many times you lose count? That's gotta be what doing it right means, yeah?"

"Yep. That's the surest way, I'd say."

"Uh huh..."

I open up the Hanon textbook. First up are the finger exercises...just like how with sports, you start off practice by warming up.

"It's 25 and 26 today, right?" I ask.

"Now this *is* strange, Takeshi. For you to be so self-motivated, I mean. What's up?"

Well, yeah. If I were my usual self, those do-re-mi-do-re-mi-fa-re-mi-fa-sol-fa-mi-sol-fa-mi finger exercises definitely wouldn't be something I'd care all that much for.

But the thought of telling Mr. Takayanagi that he was right kinda bugs me, so I keep quiet and start carefully playing the practice songs that I used to find so boring.

The entire time, I read the sheet music more carefully, more closely than usual.

"That's good. It's like I've been saying, these basic exercises help your fingers get stronger and move around faster, which is why it's so important to do them properly. It's the same as running and stretching for athletes."

"...Mm-hmm, I got it."

Mr. Takayanagi looks surprised to see me so committed and earnest. In his eyes, I never took things this seriously before. Man, that's rough.

Since then, I'm trying to take my practice more seriously. The reason is, I realized that I'm not even close to Kosei's level when it comes to making my sounds smooth and even.

I want to be able to make them the exact same quality, like Kosei does. Imagine it like a fighting game—you chain the same basic attack, hit away at your enemies' weak spots, and clear out the regular mobs.

It's like laying down a wicked barrage.

If the strength of your attacks is all over the place, they're hit or miss, and you're just mashing the buttons, and once your own HP gets low and an enemy slips through, you're toast.

That won't cut it—you've gotta lay down a perfect barrage. A barrage of notes.

Now I can picture how to become unbeatable.

Every day, I imitate Kosei by playing the Hanon practice songs for an hour, following Mr. Takayanagi's advice and trying to play two measures at a time perfectly.

After I get home from school, I play for two hours before and after dinner, practicing four hours a day. And on the weekends, I spend the hours that I would be in school practicing, too, so that makes ten hours a day at least.

No more soccer games, dumb conversations, or messing

around with my friends, no more video games or TV, no more watching clips online or comic books—I cut all of that out.

All of it, everything. I try my hardest to do without it.

It's tough turning down my friends' invitations to play soccer.

And it's tough saying no when they ask me to play video games, too.

Even when it comes to chatting at recess, just so I can focus on reading my sheet music, I slip out of the classroom and head down the stairs by myself. Leaving the classroom while I can hear everybody's voices behind me makes me feel so lonely that my chest aches, and it's really, really tough.

And even though I do all of these things...

At the next concert, I end up losing to Kosei again.

Still, I come in right behind him, finishing second place in the first round. So Mr. Takayanagi is proud of me. 'Cause my track record up to now has always been that I barely make it into the group of ten kids who pass the prelim, and then sometimes I clear the second round, sometimes not.

I'm standing in the hall foyer—in a corner of the big open area in front of the entrance to the audience seats—and looking up at the list of kids who passed the first round that's been posted to the bulletin board. That's when I feel Mr. Takayanagi put his hand on my shoulder.

"Takeshi, you worked really hard for this. See? I told you practice would pay off."

He's in a really good mood, but for some reason I don't feel so great. It's so frustrating...the feeling that I shoulda done better is boiling inside me.

"Mmm... Still got a ways to go, I guess."

"Terrific, Takeshi, finally you've got the ambition to be better. All right, what would you like as a reward if you make it through the second round?"

"...I'll think about it."

I shake his hand off me and turn my back to the list.

What I want now isn't a new Transformation Belt, or the new game console that's coming out next month, or even the kind of sports bike all my friends from school have started riding.

Before, there was always something I wanted to own.

Man, Kosei really played awesome...

His performance, filling the music hall for the competition, was totally different from the other contestants. What I mean is, even though I knew this ever since I heard his piano for the first time, to me, the smoothness of all his melodies and flawless consistency just seemed different.

Now, I can tell that every little sound that Kosei's ten fingers make stands apart from other people's, and his overall songs, the combination of those sounds, also aren't the same as other people's.

Every twinkling grain of sound that he plays, every last powerful little pellet of it—that's what I want.

But I already know that's not the kind of thing you can just beg someone to buy for you.

I pass through the automatic doors of the music hall, and as I wait for my dad to come pick me up at the drop-off area, I look at the palms of my hands again. I wiggle my ten fingers.

"To get the sound I want, I've gotta grab it with these hands, these ten fingers right here."

It'll be tough. But it's the only way.

With my eyes on the second round, I'm at my piano at least five hours every day—since I have homework to do after I get home from school, I force myself to get up early for an extra hour of morning practice. I play the same phrases over and over, shooting for total perfection, until they sound exactly like what's written on the score.

When I have a little free time, I spend it reading sheet music. I'm constantly walking around with copies of my music sheets and reading. Not just at home, but during school recess, too.

Memorizing a score isn't something I do while I'm playing the piano. First I read it, and as I'm playing the song in my head or playing air piano, I memorize all the notes and instructions written on the sheet. To help me remember, I also write things down or put highlights on the sheet. Recreating them on an actual piano is what I do in practice.

That's why once I've memorized the score, the sounds of a piano always echo perfectly inside my head, just like what's on the sheet.

That's what I play. With my ten fingers, my notes overlap with the perfect piano that's playing in my brain. I play making sure there's not even the smallest gap between the two pianos.

Over and over, day after day, I practice.

Now I'm perfect, I think. I have confidence.

Mr. Takayanagi, too, says, "Amazing, Takeshi, if you can produce this sound at the competition, you can't lose. Not even to Kosei Arima."

The second round is here... I go inside the dressing room, change into my suit—that's what I wear when I'm performing— and look into the mirror so I can put on my necktie. That instant, a weird panicky feeling hits me.

Wow...do I always look this scary?

It's like a different person's face in the mirror glaring back at me.

It's cool, no problem. I can play it. I practiced a ton, right? Here I am...the second round competition for kids 14-and-under, the set piece is something Romantic, any of the twenty-four etudes by Chopin...and I'm going with Op. 10, No. 3, in E major. I'm gonna own this.

Op. 10, No. 3, in E major—or "Farewell" to most people. That's the Chopin song I've picked.

Right now, the Chopin is echoing perfectly in my head. It has been for ten days now, the whole time.

I'm perfect...I can catch up to Kosei. I can be unbeatable. I can make my notes perfect, one after another. Ones that are good enough to beat Kosei. Ones that can match his.

The Chopin is echoing in my brain... *Gotta beat Kosei...* It begins to overlap with his Bach. Perfect sounds, one after another, one after another.

The two clash. Deep inside my ears, they clash and both fall to pieces.

Cut it out, go away! Get out, all you other notes.

Kosei's sound, the sound I wanted so bad, is messing me up now. The pounding of my heart joins our two pianos now, sounding like a scream as they crash together and shatter.

Little by little it gets louder. It's roaring inside my head. It's not perfect at all, this sound—it's all crazy.

My vision grows dark. Breathing's a struggle.

Go away!! Any sound out to ruin mine, just go away...

Go away, go away, go away, go away...

I put my hands on the mirror and gaze at my own eyes that are staring wide open. Trying to hang on before it all goes dark,

I keep glaring...and glaring...and glaring.

"GO AWAY!!"

As I cry out, I feel something rising from my stomach.

Oh no. I panic and bolt for the bathroom that's next to the dressing room.

I throw up in the sink.

I puke until my stomach's empty, and then a bitter liquid's all that comes out. I get all of that out too. My pulse still sounds fast, but the noise in my head is gone now.

My reflection in the mirror has a blank look.

Yikes, my sound, where'd my sound go?

I search for it, after it frayed in my head.

Finally, I find a piece...and then another, and another, and when I gather them all, the piano inside my head starts spinning them into a clumsy melody.

"Farewell."

It's okay. That perfect sound musta been absorbed by my body—by these ten fingers right here.

I clench my fists and turn my back to the mirror. I wipe my mouth with my handkerchief and leave the bathroom. It's almost time.

In front of the dressing room, sitting against the wall in the hallway and poring over her Chopin, is a girl in a yellow dress. Her enamel shoes are sitting neatly at her side. Her bare toe tips are peeking out from the hem of her dress.

I see this girl's face at every competition from the first round onward, and apparently she lives in the same area as me and Kosei. I think Mr. Takayanagi said she's the same year as me.

I casually peek at the score and see it's for "Farewell," the same song I'll be playing.

The bold girl is completely focused on reading the music, paying no attention to me. The score has these colorful letters scribbled all over.

"Make it linger"…"longing and going afar"…"heart-breaking"…"a single teardrop falls"…"a warm-colored sky on a spring evening"…huh?

Those kinds of directions aren't part of the original score. I guess her instructor must be teaching her some weird stuff. Just then, she notices my gaze and glares back at me.

"Got a problem?"

"Uh-uh."

Just then, someone from the staff calls out a name.

"Number five, Ms. Igawa. You're almost on."

The girl takes a deep breath.

"Yes."

She stands up still holding the score and disappears behind the door leading to the offstage area.

I stay where I am, concentrating on playing perfect sounds in my head. It'll be my turn next.

I search inside my head. From the other side of a veil, I hear the faint sound of a piano.

It's my Chopin song. My "Farewell."

It's too far away to hear clearly. It sounded closer before. Those perfect notes used to just flow and flow.

Come back, come back into my hands. You're my sound.

Switching places with the girl in the yellow dress, I get to the stage to go on sixth.

When I follow the staff's directions and go near the wing, there's a huge round of applause.

The girl passes by me, looking so satisfied.

"The way I played today…I'm sure I beat Kosei."

I'm positive I hear her mutter that.

She gives me a sideways glance. Her black eyes look sharp, but also really deep and clear.

It startles me. In that moment, the sound that I've drawn into my hands, the song I thought had soaked into my whole body, falls apart inside me and scatters.

♪

I barely made it past the second round.

Kosei came in first place—he was the third from last to perform—but I didn't have it in me to listen to him play and encourage myself for the final.

I practiced so hard, I thought I'd captured that perfect sound. But on stage where it's do or die, I was no different from how I used to sound before, back when I was cutting corners... What was it, that mood floating around on the stage? It felt overwhelming, like my whole body was being squeezed... It was different from Kosei but was making the audience forget to breathe.

Kosei's performances are always perfect, exactly like on the sheet. There are lots of "classical music fans" who don't think perfection is beautiful, though. That's the truth.

So it's rare for the mood coming from the audience to be so overwhelming. They aren't professional judges, nor professional players...the bigger "fans" they are, the stronger the tendency.

But...the mood that girl created was the kind that moved exactly those fans.

Even I was overawed by it.

I practiced so hard. I wish I could've faced Kosei alone with

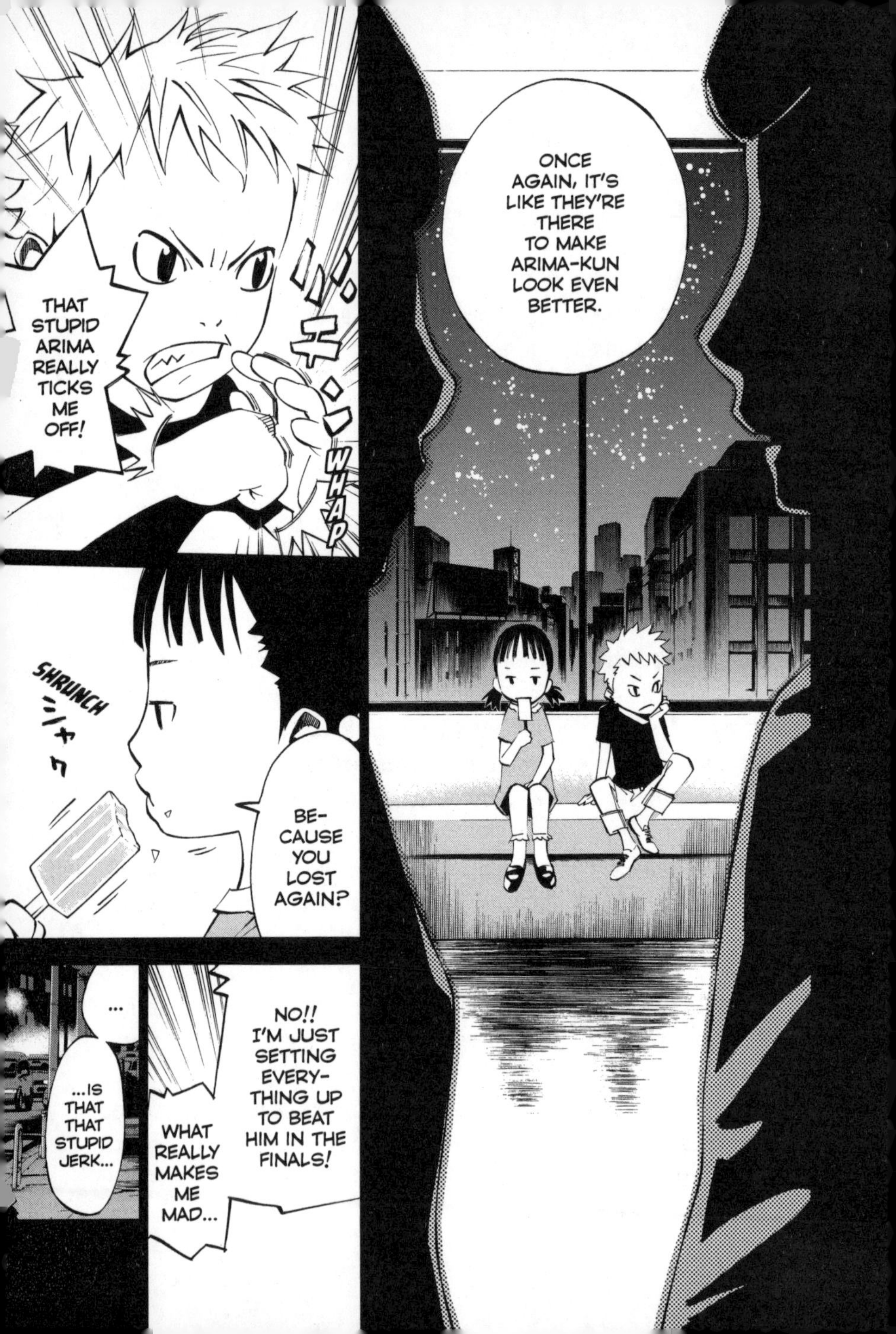
ONCE AGAIN, IT'S LIKE THEY'RE THERE TO MAKE ARIMA-KUN LOOK EVEN BETTER.
THAT STUPID ARIMA REALLY TICKS ME OFF!
WHAP
SHRUNCH
BE-CAUSE YOU LOST AGAIN?
NO!! I'M JUST SETTING EVERY-THING UP TO BEAT HIM IN THE FINALS!
WHAT REALLY MAKES ME MAD...
...
...IS THAT THAT STUPID JERK...

no audience, and no distractions!

I'm so peeved that now there's no way I could forget her name.

Emi Igawa.

A fourth grader, like me and Kosei.

She sees him as her rival according to Mr. Takayanagi.

"Takeshi, you're sulking again. I can tell you're skipping out on practice. It's been a week since the second round—you haven't played at all, have you? Don't go losing your focus just because you made it to the finals. It'll be much harder, you understand."

This is how he scolds me when our first lesson after the second competition is done.

Then, when I'm about to say goodbye, he puts a Hero Transformation Belt box in my hands.

"This is from your parents and me. You practiced really hard this time. And even though the result was the same as usual, your effort was really something else."

"...Thank you."

"Now, show me what you've got for the finals. If you don't stop Kosei, he's gonna win again. All right?"

"O-kay."

Me, stop Kosei? Nuh-uh, no way.

My teacher senses my thoughts.

"Takeshi, I mean it, you understand? If there's anyone who can reach Kosei's level and even beat him someday, it's you. I think you're the only one who knows how to win those scores from the competition judges and become unbeatable. But no matter how well the coaches know it, the players themselves have to get it deep down. And you do."

Yeah, I give a half-hearted answer. Something's not right. What *do* I want?

The piano competitions use a point-deduction scoring system.

The fair way is to judge whether or not the player played perfectly like on the music sheet.

It doesn't matter how much personal feeling you put in or how much the piece means to you or the audience, you can't turn that stuff into points and show it to other people.

That's why the player's skill at playing the song perfectly, the way it's written on the music sheet, is what gets judged. The more different your playing is from the directions, the more points get deducted.

Mr. Takayanagi's trying pretty hard to reach me.

"Your strength is that you've got real respect not only for the music, but for the composer, too—"

He looks like there's something more he wants to say, but I say a quick thank-you, bolt out the door, and head home on my bike.

When I finished playing at the second round, my head was empty.

There wasn't any sound in there at all.

Even looking at a piano just gives me this restless, unpleasant feeling that I can't explain, and I can't bring myself to open the lid. When I breathe the air by the piano, I feel like I'm suffocating.

I know the finals are coming up.

Maybe getting cut in the second round would've made things easier...

Now I have to get on stage again with that perfect sound playing in my head. The sound I wanted, the sound that used to be mine, that unbeatable sound—I've gotta pull it out from my brain, make the judges and the audience all hear it, and show 'em I'm the best.

Back to square one, huh? But my sound's gone away.

Ugh, whatta hassle.

I wish being like Kosei was easier. I wish I could play like him casually, right now.

Just then, as I'm walking along the schoolyard, I see several boys from my class through the backstop net. They're kicking and chasing after a soccer ball.

Somehow, it looks really fun. I stop my bike and watch them for a while, and when they notice I'm there, they wave and run over to me.

—Takeshi, tomorrow after school we're playing our second game against Class One. You gotta help us out here. You know K-man went home early, right? The class health monitor said he had a fever.

—He could be out tomorrow.

—Don't wanna push him too hard if he's not a hundred percent, yeah?

—This is you we're talking about, Takeshi. Just practice with us a little now and you'll be good to go.

I've been so busy with piano that I'm not socializing much these days, but some of my buddies still want me to hang out. I almost say yes.

—If there's anyone who can reach Kosei's level and even beat him someday, it's you.

In my brain, Mr. Takayanagi's words come back to life. At

the same time, the sound of a perfect piano starts playing.

It's Kosei's Bach. Da-da da-da-da da-da-da, da-da da-da-da da-da-da. Da-da da-da-da da-da-da, da-da da-da-da da-da-da. Do-mi sol-do-mi sol-do-mi, do-mi sol-do-mi, sol-do-mi.

That "Farewell"—which I'd thought was perfect—is gone now.

But Kosei's Bach is back in my head. It didn't go anywhere.

I listen to the music echoing in my brain for a while.

I wanna play perfectly too. To make everybody see. A sound that all the judges, the audience filling the hall—everybody— can see is perfect, a sound that represents the music sheet whole.

"Takeshi? What's wrong? You're spacing out."

Da-da da-da-da da-da-da, da-da da-da-da da-da-da. Da-da da-da-da da-da-da, da-da da-da-da da-da-da.

Do-re la-re-fa la-re-fa, do-re la-re-fa la-re-fa.

Kosei was practicing so many hours over and over. There's no way I can get the perfect sound skipping all the practicing that he's been doing. If I'd done it, I'd have surpassed him a long time ago.

Da-da da-da-da da-da-da, da-da da-da-da da-da-da. Da-da da-da-da da-da-da, da-da da-da-da da-da-da.

Ti-re sol-re-fa sol-re-fa, ti-re sol-re-fa, sol-re-fa.

As I listen to the sound, I stare at the palms of my hands and then squeeze them tightly. I see the faces of all my friends. Yuuki, Kento, Sho, Yocchin, Reiya, Masa, Junpei...

I...

"I'm sorry...I've gotta practice piano."

I put my hands together and apologize. "Okay..." they say, looking very disappointed, and go back to the center of the schoolyard.

I thought I'd made up my mind.

Once I face the piano, my friends playing soccer flickers on the back of my eyelids.

They looked like they were having fun. Without K-man, they might lose to Class One...

"Dammit, what do I really want?!" I shout. Then the sound echoes in my brain.

Da-da da-da-da da-da-da, da-da da-da-da da-da-da. Da-da da-da-da da-da-da, da-da da-da-da da-da-da. Do-mi, sol-do-mi, sol-do-mi, do-mi, sol-do-mi, sol-do-mi. Do-re la-re-fa la-re-fa, do-re la-re-fa la-re-fa.

I play the same song. I let all my ten fingers dance on the keyboard.

But when they touch the piano and the actual sound reaches my ears, I can't ignore the gap between the two sounds. No matter how many times I play they don't even overlap, and it gets hard to breathe.

It's getting to be too much, and then I picture my friends' faces and start worrying about tomorrow's soccer match.

"No, I gotta play piano, that's what I've decided. I know Kosei's making an effort, and I know I need to try harder. If I go to sleep tonight without practicing at all, of course there's no way I'm gonna wake up tomorrow and be the best...I know that!"

But I don't really know. Would it be fun being the best? Would it feel great? If I became the best, would I not feel confused?

Frustrated, I stand up and start pacing in the piano room, looking all around. I notice the square-shaped bump in the backpack that I always wear to my lessons. It's the Transformation Belt.

"I didn't do it 'cause I wanted this."

I pull the belt out of my bag together with the box, go to my room, and stuff the thing into the drawer underneath my bed. I don't even open the box.

I don't need new toys anymore. I'm bold enough to say no to my friends.

I just want that perfect sound.

The perfect sound...what does it mean?

Da-da da-da-da da-da-da, da-da da-da-da da-da-da. Da-da da-da-da da-da-da, da-da da-da-da da-da-da. Do-mi sol-do-mi sol-do-mi, do-mi sol-do-mi sol-do-mi. Do-re la-re-fa la-re-fa, do-re la-re-fa la-re-fa.

The sound of the piano in my brain, what is it really? Is it perfect?

Why does it feel so...hard to breathe?

Didn't I always feel this way? Ever since I stopped playing with my friends and started practicing really hard four or five hours a day, and ten hours on the weekends. I've just been pretending not to notice.

I leave home, and bike on over to Kosei's house. The only sound I admire is Kosei's. I wanna hear his real sound. The sound he works so hard at.

Riding on an embankment along the river, I spot some kids horsing around on the bridge going across the water.

"Hey...that's Kosei."

I hold my breath and stop pedaling.

He's having fun with a shorthaired girl. They're diving into the river from the bridge rail over and over again. The other kids are hooting and hollering, too.

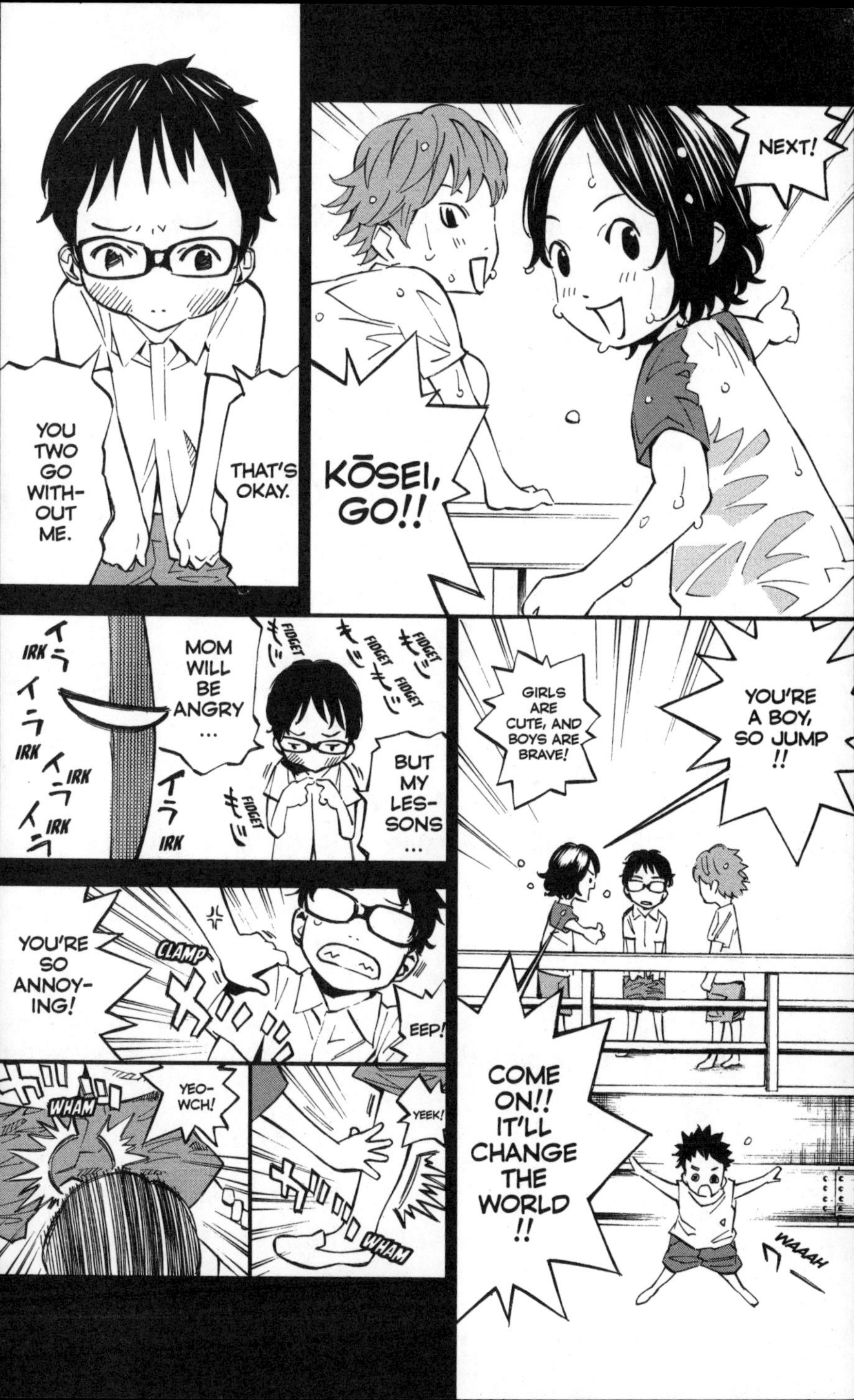

NEXT!
KŌSEI, GO!!
THAT'S OKAY.
YOU TWO GO WITH-OUT ME.
YOU'RE A BOY, SO JUMP!!
GIRLS ARE CUTE, AND BOYS ARE BRAVE!
COME ON!! IT'LL CHANGE THE WORLD!!
WAAAH
FIDGET FIDGET FIDGET FIDGET
MOM WILL BE ANGRY...
BUT MY LES-SONS...
IRK IRK IRK IRK IRK
YOU'RE SO ANNOY-ING!
CLAMP
EEP!
YEEK!
WHAM
YEO-WCH!
WHAM

Kosei plunges down with a huge splash. As the water sprays all around him, little particles of light burst as well.

"Wha..."

What the? Wait...huh?

He's...Kosei's playing with his friends? Why's he laughing so much?

I stand there stunned for a while, still straddling my bike.

He comes out onto the riverbed soaking wet, cackling and smiling with the other kids who seem to be his friends. He wipes his wet forehead and cheeks with the backs of his hands.

...Kosei is having fun, like an ordinary kid.

The dipping, golden sun is reflecting off the surface of the river. It'll be autumn soon.

All of a sudden, I feel like I can hear music coming from the sparkling river. It's Kosei's piano and his even notes. It's also coming from the autumn wind shaking the blades of grass on the riverbed, from the shiny puffs of clouds in the sky that's starting to change from blue to yellow.

I want to laugh now, too. So I do. All by myself.

I laugh and laugh, and then take a deep breath.

It feels like the air reaches to the bottom of my belly, for the first time in so long. The autumn air is a little chilly.

The next day, I go around to all my friends asking to play, and they let me in the soccer match against Class One after school.

I don't score, but I have a couple of assists, and one of them nets a goal.

The whole time during the match, that beautiful piano sound with its even notes, crystal clear, echoes from deep inside me.

My body feels so light somehow.

I shout out loud, cheering my friends on.

I run as fast as I can from corner to corner on the field.

We win the match three to one.

When I get home, I'm gonna start playing piano again tonight—with this lighter body of mine.

♯ 2 〚 ♪ Kosei's a Liar 〛 Emi Igawa

Ever since that day, I keep on getting betrayed by Kosei.

Trusting him might've been a mistake, but Kosei...the Kosei I see now, that's not the real him. Absolutely no way.

Why? Why does nobody notice—not even Kosei himself?

It's autumn, and I'm a fifth grader.

I'm at the concert hall for the district preliminary of the Saiki Piano Competition.

I'm looking at the monitor back stage, thinking the same thing over and over as I stare at Kosei's hands playing the piano. He got picked to go last, as a seeded contestant, because he'd won the competition last year as the youngest winner.

He betrayed me again. Why is he doing this? It's just gonna make the audience dislike him even more. He should just go back to being the Kosei he used to be. Why's he always gotta act the bad guy? Is it fun to play the villain?

Kosei keeps playing perfectly. He's doing a Haydn sonata—the Piano Sonata in A major, Hob. XVI: 26, 1st movement, Allegro moderato. We all had to pick a set piece song in the classical style, one of the designated sonatas by Haydn, Mozart, or Beethoven.

I remember that at the final round of the Nagai Memorial Competition last month, too, he played Haydn's Piano Sonata No. 43 in E flat major, Hob. XVI, Finale, and won without making any mistakes. I've been so focused on the Saiki Piano Competition that I didn't take part in that one.

He picks the hardest songs on purpose, ones the other kids would never, and plays them perfectly to snatch first place. That's been Kosei over the past six months...after he got to fifth grade. Without taking any breaks, he shows up at every competition, and just about every month he gets another certificate for passing a prelim, another championship award, or another trophy.

"The trophy thief"—that's what he's called these days.

"Emi? There you are."

It's my piano teacher Yuriko Ochiai. She comes over to me.

"You're watching Kosei again, aren't you? Does he bother you so much?"

"...Yes."

"And since he picked a different song from yours, it's bothering you even more. Why do you care so much about winning with the same song he's playing?"

"Do you think I can beat him?"

She gives me a vague smile, and only says, "Do your best." It's been this way for a long time, like for a few years.

"I didn't think he was gonna play Haydn again. I was sure he'd choose Beethoven's Op. 27 No. 2, 3rd movement. That song's really intense, so he can show off his techniques."

That's why I played that piece.

I'd practiced really hard, and I created my own image for it. Even after I checked the program and realized that we'd picked different songs, my passion didn't go away—it still drove me on. Like a tempest, harder, faster and faster, I pulled off the distinctive arpeggios like I was in a frenzy.

It frustrated me that I couldn't fight him head-on, but I played with my whole heart, showing them how much I wanted to beat Kosei and how intense my passion for piano was.

My piece—the 3rd movement of Beethoven's Piano Sonata No. 14 in C sharp minor, Op. 27 No. 2, Presto agitato. The popular name for it is "Moonlight Sonata."

You hear the calming 1st movement of "Moonlight Sonata" a lot on TV as background music. The "da-la-la, da-la-la" is played by the left hand, accompanying the main melody that goes "duum, dah, da-duum," which is played by the right hand. This 1st movement is a favorite for people who just enjoy playing piano once in a while.

For competitions, more technically difficult songs get chosen. The 3rd movement is perfect for a set piece because it has just the right amount of difficulty and intensity. Presto agitato—*play faster, and harder*—that's what Beethoven says.

...Kosei finishes playing Haydn's sonata and bows to the judges and the audience. He gets a round of applause. But not like the one I got—not *that* loud.

For me, the audience was so excited and their clapping showed more enthusiasm. The entire hall was far more filled with applause.

There was a sparkle in their eyes. But now—for Kosei? I don't think so, no way.

"That was a splendid Haydn, following the sheet completely and with no mistakes. He's like a machine... Oh, I guess you've already heard this hundreds of times. I'm tired of saying it, too."

Miss Ochiai gives a wry smile. I bite my lips. Now I'm way madder.

Why didn't he choose "Moonlight"? Even right this minute, I want him to do it over, with my song. And I wanna know which one of us gets applauded more, excites the audience more.

I played with my whole heart, with all the energy I had. I felt so high until I finished playing and got applauded. But now, I feel empty...

"Emi, you really are upset, aren't you? Just because you guys played different songs..."

"Do you think I could've won if he'd played the same song? I mean, in my performance today, I played so hard and with so much energy that it made me feel really good. It was strong like a scream, but also soft like a whisper."

My teacher looks away from me and also changes the subject. "Competitions are difficult, you know. If you played Beethoven all the time, they might think that's all you knew. Even when Chopin is supposed to be your set piece, and you don't have a choice, they get tired of hearing just Chopin. No matter what you play, they've adopted this cold, harsh mindset, and the hurdle keeps getting higher. A 'trophy thief' has to face those voices, too. In fact, there was a pianist in Europe who was called that, and at one competition, he ended up in second place even though his techniques were the best. What do you think he did at the gala concert?"

"Did he boycott it?"

The teacher shakes her head, and after confirming my reaction, answers, "Instead of the designated song in the program, he played a very famous one that everybody knows. Even people who aren't into classical music have heard at least its first theme."

A song everybody knows...what? "Für Elise"? "Traumerei"? I can't come up with the answer.

"Which one?"

She tells me with a straight face, "Chopin's Piano Sonata No. 2, 3rd movement."

"...Oh, 'The Funeral March'!"

The familiar song instantly plays in my ears. Dum-dah-da-duum, dah-da, dah-da, dah-da, duum.

"That's so sarcastic."

"Right?" my teacher says, chuckling.

I feel like I want to play "The Funeral March," too.

I know it'll be Kosei who comes in first, while second place will probably go to Takeshi Aiza.

Takeshi used to be an okay player but started getting a lot better since last winter, and at the Maiho Music Competition held between summer and autumn this year, he breezed all the way through to the final. He nabbed one of the top spots, even if it was the lowest one. Up until then, even getting through the second round was hit or miss for him.

It was Kosei who came in first.

For me it's always the same. This past year or so, it's like the third-place spot for our district's been reserved for me, behind Kosei and Takeshi. Before that, I was going back and forth between second and fourth place. So when Takeshi shot past me, sure, it kinda bothered me, but Kosei's been my only rival.

Still, I didn't forget to glare at Takeshi.

But today, I didn't even get to face off against Kosei. 'Cause we ended up picking different songs. So there was no way the audience could compare us.

Even worse, this was twice in a row that we went with different songs.

Next time, I've gotta be more careful with my guessing.

"Okay then, let's go," Miss Ochiai urges. "That's it for the first round."

When Miss Ochiai and I go out to the open foyer in the hall, Takeshi starts talking to me. He's already changed out of the suit he was wearing for the performance, and now he's dressed in something loose and casual.

"Oh, Emi. The results have been posted. They came out pretty fast this time."

He points to a corner of the list. Ever since he made a habit of coming in second behind Kosei, he's started talking to me more. I have no idea why.

"Okay."

I look up at the list hanging on the wall showing who qualified. I'm in third place, just like I figured. First Kosei, then Takeshi, then me. I'm sure it'll be the same thing in the second round. If Takeshi makes a mistake and I don't screw up, we might switch places, but it'll still be Kosei in first place. I can already see myself being disappointed in the final.

That's the level that the judges think I, Emi Igawa, am at right now.

How come you gotta play exactly what's on the sheet, like a machine, to win these competitions?

Is that the only standard these judges go by?

You can fill the song with emotions and a message, express yourself by playing with all your heart and soul, and even move and touch your audience, making your sound linger in their hearts, but none of it will help your score.

Emotion doesn't translate into numbers. Because everybody has a totally different way of feeling.

But I can't accept that.

I believe piano should be something that moves you.

It was Kosei who first moved me with his playing.

Kosei, who's the same age as me. I encountered his piano for the first time when I was five.

One Sunday at the end of summer, I was invited to a concert that a preschool buddy of mine was going to be in. I didn't know what it was, I just went.

Thinking back to it now, it must have been a recital organized by private piano tutors who'd rented the hall together. Most of the performers were preschool to elementary. The girls looked so happy to have a chance to wear a frilly princess dress, and the songs they played were just arrangements of anime theme songs and pop hits.

Even the anime songs I knew got boring when the recital turned out to be two hours long. I'd almost fallen asleep when Kosei showed up on stage.

The song he played was so cheerful and fun and energetic, it seemed to twinkle.

But it wasn't only cheerful—sometimes it got gloomy, too, like when the sun gets covered up by thin clouds. The melody was somehow sweet but also a little bitter, and it stayed in your mind.

I didn't even know the name of the song at the time. I found out about three years after I started playing piano. One day my teacher said, "How about we do this one next?" and played it for me. That was the one.

Mozart's Piano Sonata No. 3 in B flat major, K. 281, 3rd movement, Allegro (rondo).

The song has a radiance to it—like a flower garden in midsummer, where all the flowers are blooming proudly for all their lives' worth, and the sun's shining down on them—and also this light shadow that's sweet and sad and sort of tickles your heart. That kind of mood is unique to Mozart.

When Kosei played it, it seemed like so much fun, he seemed to love playing piano, to love its vibrant tones. That's what came across to me, and every single note sparkled.

When he finished playing, the music lingered and seeped into the audience.

I didn't want the sound to fade away—the beautiful shiny sound, the wonderful tones that bounced with joy and yet wrapped around you gently. It felt like I was surrounded by lovely flowers, enchanted by their scent, and it amazed me how that feeling stayed inside me. My heart wouldn't slow down, and somehow I just couldn't hold it in anymore. My eyes welled up with tears, and all my feelings burst out at once, and I started bawling.

I was just...so moved.

The piano playing of five-year-old Kosei Arima embodied the joy of music.

That was it.

I wanted to play the piano like him.

I wanted strangers to be touched profoundly by my performances.

That Sunday...I let go of a future of endless possibilities.

When I got home that evening, with my eyes red from

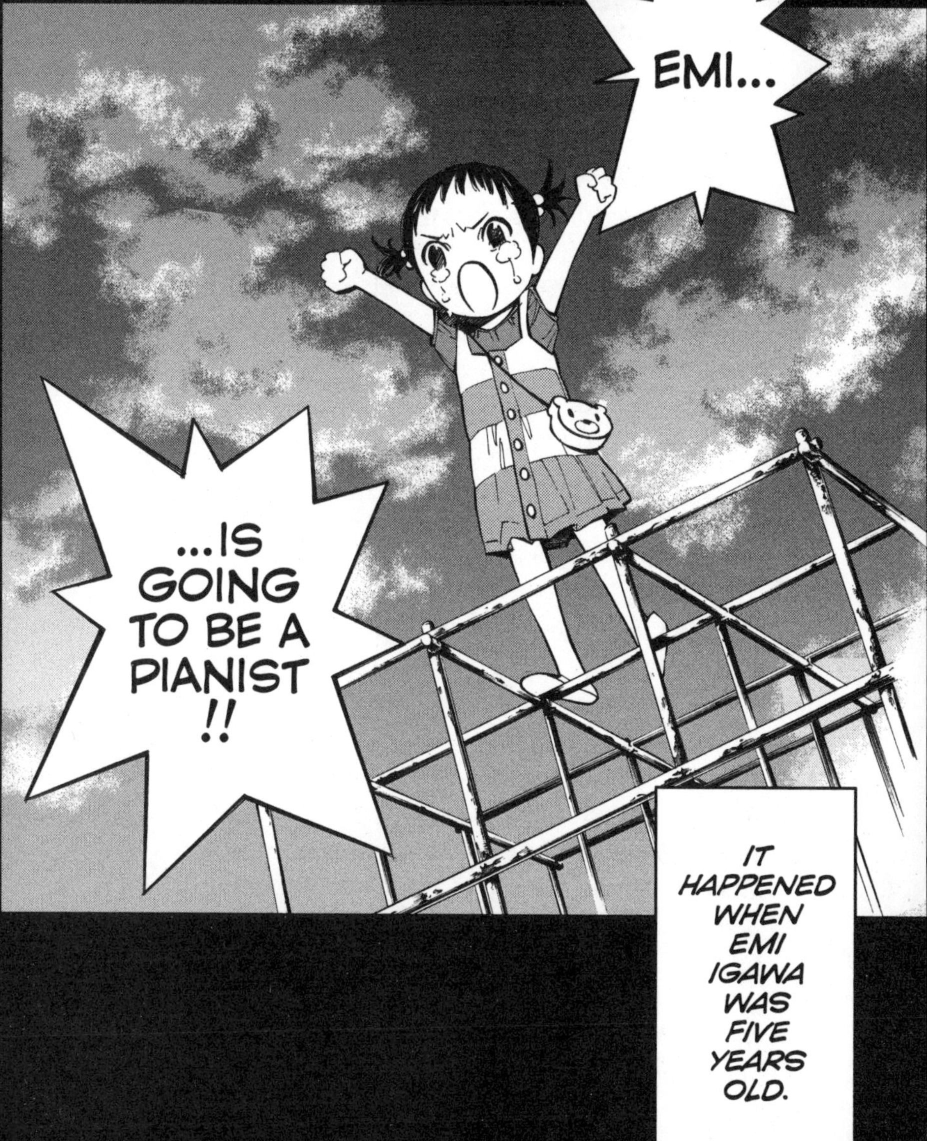
EMI...
...IS GOING TO BE A PIANIST!!
IT HAPPENED WHEN EMI IGAWA WAS FIVE YEARS OLD.

crying, I took my parents out under the rosy sky. They tried to keep me under control but I shook free and went to the highest spot that I could climb to by myself at the time—the top of the jungle gym in the children's park near our house. I thrust my hands toward the red sky and shouted at the top of my lungs.

"Emi is going to be a pianist!!"

One after another, noticing that the results of the first round have been posted, the other players start filling the foyer. They'd been lurking in corners, anxious to see how they did.

—I made it!

—Uh, I knew it.

—I wish my fingers hadn't slipped at that one part and screwed me up...

—All right! Finally made it to the second round!

At competitions, there's a golden rule:

Don't make mistakes.

Only people who avoid making the kind of big, obvious mistakes that knock down their score have their names put up, and even then, they have to see themselves ranked.

The area in front of the results is jammed with kids, some thrilled, some disappointed. When I step away, Takeshi follows me and says something.

"Anyway, we did a good job, Emi."

Miss Ochiai quietly slips away. I spin around to look for her and see her signaling with her eyes. She wants me to talk to Takeshi?

"Kosei won again," he says. "Perfect and flawless like always, right?"

For some reason he sounds so glad when he says it that it ticks me off. I can't help sounding aggressive when I answer him. "Excuse me, but aren't you upset?"

"Relax. Of course I'm upset, but I figure there'll be more chances to compete. Let's just say I've still got him in my sights."

"So he's your target."

"Say, Emi, you and Kosei didn't play the same piece this time. Seems like you guys always do."

"...I try to. I guessed wrong this time."

Takeshi blinks at me, looking confused. "You mean, you do it on purpose? Whoa, that's ballsy. When it happens to me I get freaked out. It'd be so obvious—how much more he practices, I mean."

"When I hear your piano, Takeshi, no matter how you play, it never makes me sad. But with Kosei, the more perfectly he plays, the sadder I get. Like it hurts to listen to. Don't you think so?"

He tilts his head. "You can think whatever you want when you're playing, but in the end what matters is whether you play it right. Sure, the amount you practice or the shape you're in can affect how you sound...but Kosei's playing doesn't sound painful to me."

"It's like he's saying, 'I'm trying hard so accept me. I'm doing my best to play like it says on the sheet, I'm not thinking about anything else, I'm not adding anything that doesn't belong or leaving anything out.' He's saying being correct is all that matters. He doesn't have any thoughts or strong feelings about the song, and there's nothing he wants to say through it, nothing at all."

His mother's puppet, a robot doing just what his mama tells him, an unfeeling slave to the sheet music—those are the things that the audience says about the "trophy thief" Kosei.

Apparently, his mom majored in piano at a music college and studied under a famous professor.

She couldn't make it as a professional pianist and ended up teaching at a music school. She pushed her failed dream—of flying around the world as a pro—onto her son, or at least that's the rumor among the people who come to the competitions.

I only happened to hear that recently, too. But it has nothing to do with why I hate the way he plays ever since he started elementary school.

I just can't stand to listen to him now.

His playing doesn't shine or sparkle. And no light means there's no shadow, either. It's totally flat, and it's got nothing you can grab onto, like a surface you just skid on.

He tries his best. He plays the song correctly. If the sheet music says *pianissimo*, he touches the keys gently. If it says *sforzando*, he hits the key especially hard on just that note. He's careful to play the smooth slurs differently from the sharp staccatos, and he steps on his damper pedal to hold his notes, just like the symbols say. For him it's like, *I have to play correctly, just like the sheet music tells me, don't I? I'm not thinking about anything I shouldn't be...* That's how boring his playing is. It's so stiff that I feel suffocated just listening to it.

That's it—his playing tells me he's not enjoying it at all!

There's no sense at all that he loves piano and wants to share that love with his audience.

If his playing let you know he had a fire in him to win, it wouldn't be so suffocating.

I say, "Maybe he does wanna be a machine with no feelings."

"Nah...that can't be, can it? I mean, he's human. I've seen him playing with his friends and stuff. He was laughing."

Takeshi sounds confident, but it's news to me.

"Then that's even worse! He can play piano like it's so much fun, he can make his sound come alive, all sparkly and shiny—I know he can. You don't know the real Kosei, do you, Takeshi? His playing during his first recital, back when he was five, that was the real him...but he's turning into a machine! A robot just spitting the music sheet back out!"

Takeshi smiles, surprised. "The real Kosei, huh? The only Kosei I know is the one who doesn't make mistakes. Okay, say he stops only playing what's on the sheet like he does now and inserts his own interpretations into his piano. Even if he does that, he's built up his techniques so much that he knows all the little ways he's gotta be careful so the judges can't dock him. Then he'd really be unbeatable, you know? Just means I gotta work harder."

See you next time, Takeshi says with a raised hand. He goes through the automatic door in the lobby, with its glass walls that go all the way up to the ceiling. He walks towards the footbridge crossing over the rotary in front of the station. I see a couple of people who must be his parents standing on the bridge and waving at him.

As he goes off, Miss Ochiai comes over to me.

"I wonder how Takeshi improved so quickly? He also looks like he's gotten taller. I guess that's how it is with boys. They grow so fast, if you blink you'll miss it, as they say."

I don't get what that means, but as she says it she takes her cell phone out of her bag and turns it on. At competitions, they ask you to keep it on silent.

"Oh, I got an email from your parents, Emi... They're waiting in the parking lot. Time to go home. Don't forget your bag, and put on your coat or you'll catch cold out there."

♪

At the second prelim, I guess right. I see in the event program that Kosei and I picked the same piece. I'm so excited I could shout.

The options were the same as in the first round, but we had to pick a different one from last time. He and I are both going with Beethoven's Piano Sonata No. 23 in F minor, Op. 57, 3rd movement, Allegro ma non troppo—better known as the 3rd movement of the "Appassionata."

At competitions, it's pretty common for Kosei to play something by Beethoven at least once if it's an option. This time, he played Haydn in the first round, so I was sure he'd do Beethoven for the second...because in the final, we have to play one of the songs we did in the prelims, while the other one can be whatever we want.

That's how I guessed. The judges chose fifteen out of Beethoven's many sonatas (well, one movement from each), so I listened to them all, checked the scores side by side, and then very, very carefully picked my song.

Nailed it.

The same song. "Appassionata," 3rd movement.

Even if I can't place first, even if I get ranked under Kosei by the judges like always, the audience will know for sure which of our performances touched their hearts more.

That's how I can show them Kosei's way is wrong.

I don't expect anything from the judges anymore. If I do, they'll just disappoint me. There's nothing I can do about the fact that there's no other way to score us.

But I have a lot of other people, the audience filling the hall, on my side.

The size of their applause means they admire my piano and reject Kosei for playing like a machine.

I practiced hard over and over.

Allegro ma non troppo, instructs the 3rd movement of "Appassionata"—fast, but not too fast.

Still, there's a hidden passion worthy of its nickname running through the song.

Passion—exactly the message I want to send. I want my feelings for piano to knock over the audience, and Kosei especially. I just wanna make them know that piano is a way to express passion and it should always be used to move people.

Forcefully...gently...forcefully then gently...tenderly yet intensely... That's how I'm gonna play. I'm gonna make a sound that's all my own.

With my image complete, I'm ready for the second round.

Kosei's going last this time too, and I'm on right before him.

"This is the best stage. I'm so excited, I'm shaking."

I say this to Miss Ochiai and then go on stage, actually trembling. I sit down, facing the black piano that's there all by itself under the spotlight.

My playing starts off smoothly, with my wrists still nice and flexible. My fingers go right where I want them to be.

They're dancing, wandering between the white keys and black keys, moving fluidly to the left and right on the row of keys.

My sounds are nice and loud, too. I'm calm enough that the strong ones and the soft ones are both coming through clearly.

Very nice.

My ideal sound resonates. My fingers, my hands, my body

are creating a sound that's my own.

This is my piano. Go on, listen.

I get past the part where the main melody switches from left to right and back to left, and then comes a whole rest. I put all my feeling into that silence.

Then there's a chord played with the left hand that makes the silence stand out more—that's where I make a mistake. All sound, including noise from the audience, has ceased, and enjoying it, I wonder, *Did I stretch the rest out too long?*

I forget to do the natural with my left hand on the next chord. I touch a black key. Right away I slide my finger to tap the white key, and the next moment I feel my heart pounding louder.

Then the *pianissimo* with just my right hand—is the sound not resonating? Now the half notes with my left hand. The way it sounds when I'm playing with only one hand makes me uneasy. I need a chord.

But the chord I wanted comes out muddy because my right pinky misses the key.

My passion is cooling. Anxiety takes its place.

Should I have played faster?

Should I have played louder and louder?

All of a sudden the keyboard feels chilly.

What felt as warm as my body temperature is so cold now and heavy, like it's a totally different thing.

I've lost the connection between the piano and me.

What am I gonna do?

It feels like the sound I owned is slipping away freely through my fingers.

This piano won't express my passion. I have no control anymore, it's not singing with me. No matter how much passion

I put in, it won't get any better.

Should I have played more insistently as if to knock on people's hearts?

Should I have played with a lighter touch, like a whisper?

Still confused, without recovering the passion that I meant to put into the song, or the connection that I had with the piano, I finish playing.

The applause is loud. But it's not what they gave me for the first round.

—She couldn't take the pressure.

—She got a little drunk on herself.

—I thought she played better than that.

—It was rickety, too strong or too soft at times.

—No, in the last part, she didn't differentiate the strong and soft taps enough.

I feel like I can hear the audience muttering their carefree views. Everybody's giving me a cold look...

...It's all in my head, it's all in my head, it's all in my head...

When I go offstage, all Miss Ochiai says is, "Good job."

Oh, so that's all she can say...

My knees go wobbly. When they bend I almost fall, but my teacher grabs my right wrist in a flash.

"Oww!"

"Emi? Does your wrist hurt? You didn't notice until now?"

I clench my teeth and nod.

It didn't bother me during the performance. Well, actually, I did feel a slight pain whenever I practiced for too long. But I pretended like it didn't hurt. Otherwise, I wouldn't be able to play.

I'd miss my chance to show who I am to the crowd.

I'd miss my chance to reject Kosei.

"I think you should ice it, and make sure to go see a doctor tomorrow. All right?"

Kosei comes on stage after I've stepped down.

In the end, Kosei nabbed first place with ease to pass the second round. But I only found this out later. I don't know whether the applause he got was bigger than mine. That's because my parents, who were sitting in the audience, came over and found out and took me right away to a doctor they know.

I have tenosynovitis—that's what the doctor says—from practicing too much. It has something to do with my hands growing a lot faster at my age.

So Kosei wins the Saiki Competition two years in a row, and I have to give up playing at the Zenkyo Competition in the winter.

While I'm recovering, my hands become bigger, and my fingers are wide enough to easily reach one octave of keys. I'm getting taller, too.

Meanwhile, Kosei has won two competitions including the Zenkyo, and he finishes in one of the top spots at the Urie International Competition, where most of the players are from overseas. This makes the second time, after last year.

It seems like the "trophy thief" is becoming more and more infamous. But there's no player around his age in Japan who's good enough to beat him. Takeshi's getting better little by little, squeezing his way into the top spots at the finals after Kosei, but that's about it.

My comeback starts in the summer of sixth grade, from the

prelims of the Maiho Competition.

I pick my piece with all the resolve you'd imagine.

The options include Beethoven sonatas, like last time.

Checking the list, though, most of the songs are different from the ones at the Saiki Competition last year, which also featured Beethoven's sonatas. Only one's the same—the 3rd movement of "Moonlight." I choose one from among twelve.

Beethoven's Piano Sonata No. 8 in C minor, Op. 13, 1st movement—the 1st movement of the so-called "Pathetique." The melody starts out sorrowful and goes on that way, true to the nickname "Pathetique" that the young Beethoven came up with. Then it turns into a melody full of poignant sentiment.

Right again.

Kosei picks it, too.

Before I even start practicing, I read the music sheet over and over to develop and complete my image.

One part sounds sorrowful, and another sounds furiously angry. I put words on the sheet, remembering my own experiences—how I felt when I was sad, how I felt when I was angry.

Like, when the soda-flavored ice candy I love was sold out and they only had the milk flavor and the chocolate flavor. But I wanted the soda flavor! Okay, so that's the smallest sorrow and anger...

Bigger sorrow: Kosei's betrayal.

Bigger anger: also Kosei's betrayal.

The anger and sadness I feel at every competition when I listen to his piano.

I practice and practice over and over. I just play piano so hard.

Anger that comes from loss and anger in the face of absurd

suffering are different. The playing shouldn't sound like I'm punching the keyboard just because I'm mad.

It's gotta resonate with the anger everybody feels for one reason or another.

I put all my sorrow, love, and bitterness into the piece, and it becomes a story. I try to play it so that it has breadth and depth. Not just strongly and boldly, but also softly and tenderly, like I'm petting the keyboard.

I read the music sheet again, making my image swell up.

And I play. I play and play, nonstop.

I sleep on a futon under my piano. I want my body to absorb all the reverberations remaining in the room, all my own passion that's soaked into the walls with the sound.

The day of the first round...my turn to go on comes right before Kosei's.

They have seats for the players on the stage wing. Five folding chairs are lined up, and we can wait our turn there, but few of us do. That's because hearing the performances gets distracting and you start thinking too much. Usually, it's okay if you're there by the time the second person ahead of you is done playing.

If the person ahead of you plays really well, you'll get depressed thinking you can't play like that, and if he or she fails, you'll feel anxious thinking that you're gonna fail, too.

In the separate waiting areas for boys and girls—depending on the hall, the backstage rooms for actors, or meeting rooms with mirrors put in there—some of us read our scores or do image training. Outside in the hallway, others try to relax by rolling their necks or shoulders or by doing stretches. Some stroll back and forth or do whatever they think brings them good luck. There are all kinds of people here. It's not uncommon to see guardians—usually parents—following them around.

Some people get pretty nervous as soon as it's their turn to play and walk onto the stage clumsily and can barely bow to the audience. Others, relaxed enough to make out the audience's faces at first, begin playing smoothly, but the second they think it's going fine, the sweat starts pouring off them and their hands start shaking. It depends on the person, and sometimes the same person will behave differently at a different competition.

But everybody—every one of us—struggles with the pressure, and our tension at the max, we play our pieces trying our best not to screw up.

We don't wanna make mistakes, so we practice over and over.

Everybody feels the same way.

I do, and probably Kosei does, too.

There I am—still looking at the sheet music even after moving to one of the folding chairs at the end of the stage, building up my image—when my name gets called. This is my moment to be in the spotlight.

As I fix the hem of my new blue dress, I stand and step forward, and out of the corner of my eye I catch a glimpse of Kosei, who's sitting on a folding chair. His posture's totally straight. He already looks like a machine, even before he starts playing. Every part of him is like a machine, a robot without emotions.

Having him in sight makes the flame in my heart flare up.

Kosei, listen to my sound, listen to my piano! I'll make you fall in love with it! Real piano—I'll make you realize what piano really means, so you'll get serious about it!

My frustration when I couldn't play piano for months, my joy that I can once again, my worries and hopes for the future— I pour all the different emotions bubbling up from the bottom of my heart into my playing.

Let my sound resonate.

Let my heart reach theirs.

Let me shine.

On the eighty-eight keys of the piano, my ten fingers run, and dance, and moan, and sing, and shout.

The piano echoes and spreads, answering my commands.

This is me!

My sound, and my passion, fills up the entire hall. It wraps every member of the audience and soaks into them.

Hear me!

Let it ring in your hearts!

This is who I am!

See? Piano is amazing, isn't it?

Piano is beautiful, piano is fantastic. Piano can express everything that I am!

Listen!

Let it echo on and on!

I love piano, 'cause it lets me express myself!

The last notes quietly melt into the audience.

The sound lingers...there's a moment of silence, and then the hall bursts into applause. Some people even give me a standing ovation.

I'm really proud of myself, and for the first time, I give a smile on stage.

I'm sure Kosei won't get this much applause, or this much praise! My sound, my passion, reached everybody.

I bow deeply and return to the wing.

I glare at Kosei, who's sitting in his chair.

He keeps his eyes lightly shut, not moving his body at all, like a doll. He's not even trying to look at me, and he doesn't feel me staring at him, doesn't budge.

He didn't feel anything from my playing?

Then...I feel sorry for him.

I'm surprised when that thought pops up in my mind.

Am I pitying him?

I am, I think he's wasting his talent. What a pity that he doesn't try to win applause, that he won't be told that his piano is moving.

He's missing out.

He could get them if he really wanted to, but he's not trying. He's definitely wasting his talent.

Sure...he's doing it to get first place, but what's he really thinking, deep down? Why is he playing piano? Did he lose who he really is...his love for piano? Why? Since when?

Kosei, you *do* love playing piano...don't you?

I pass the Maiho preliminary in second place, which is my best result for this competition that I play every year. Takeshi comes in third place. It's been a while since I last beat him.

Right before the results went up, I ran into Takeshi in the hallway in front of the waiting room. When we went to the foyer to see the results, people were groaning for some reason.

Well, it had to be because Kosei had come in first place as usual and people didn't like it.

I'd put everything into my performance, no regrets, and was able to think that.

Kosei participates in the Shirase Competition half a month later, plays Mozart, and wins. But there's a rumor that after he finished, he caused some trouble at the foyer before the results went up. He had an argument with his mother or something like that...

I don't know the details. I can't focus on my piano if I care about rumors—they just drag everybody down.

For the Maiho Competition final, too, I practice very hard so I don't lose my rank. Some tough rivals come through the preliminaries from other places.

I'm gonna roll right over them and reject Kosei even more.

The song I pick for the final is Chopin's Piano Impromptu No. 4 in C sharp minor, Op. 66, Allegro agitato—also known as "Fantaisie-Impromptu."

I want something aggressive, something that would tear and shake me up, so that I can play with feeling and put my all into it.

But.

On the day of the final, I get the program as soon as I arrive at the competition hall, impatiently flip through it, and cry, "I wanted Kosei to play this song so much last year, why now?!"

He's chosen Beethoven again. I was expecting he wouldn't, that's why I chose Chopin!

At least if we'd chosen the same Chopin, the audience could easily compare our playing...

He picked the 3rd movement of Beethoven's Piano Sonata No. 14 in C sharp minor, Op. 27 No. 2, Presto agitato—or the 3rd movement of the "Moonlight Sonata." It's the piece I played in the first round of the Saiki Competition last year.

The one where I couldn't get to face off against him.

But it's gonna be okay, I tell myself.

If it were Mozart, it'd really be hopeless. Chopin supposedly didn't release "Fantaisie-Impromptu" in his lifetime because the style turned out to be kind of similar to "Moonlight." Both songs have the direction Agitato. *So the audience at least ought to be able to compare which piano is more agitated.*

"Okay...we'll see how Kosei plays it. I know how I'm gonna play—aggressively, more and more aggressively, enough to show them how I feel!"

At the final, I'm set to play last. And ahead of the player before me is Kosei, who's playing third from last.

I'm in the monitor room with Takeshi, who's already finished playing a Mozart sonata and changed into his casual clothes. We're watching Kosei's performance on-screen.

"Moonlight," 3rd movement, Presto agitato. Play faster, more intensely.

Kosei's fingers press the keys precisely. They move to the higher sounds, and to the lower sounds, without any wasted motions. He never raises his hand up all dramatically or holds a sound too long when he should let it go—the sort of act you might put on to make yourself look "competent."

Kosei, the same as always.

He doesn't even show a fraction of an ounce of feeling. His tempo never goes wrong, not even by 0.1 seconds. Even with a fermata, where you can prolong the sound as long as you like, it sounds like it's timed... It's like he's got a rule that if it's quarter notes, he makes it three times as long as a quarter note.

"Isn't it a little too fast? It's precise, though..."

Just when Takeshi mutters this, the performance stumbles, unexpectedly.

It's where his right hand starts playing the main melody. The trill, which is supposed to make the sound twinkle finely like an ornament made with all different colors of tiny gems, slows down. Wait, no—it didn't slow down, he hit the key so hard that the sound was too loud. His finger did come away from the keyboard that much later.

"What?" Takeshi gets closer to the screen. "He's playing faster and faster? The sound...it's too loud. He's not making it quieter for the decrescendo. Like he's unable to control it."

Something's wrong, Takeshi says, frowning and crossing his arms.

It sounds so irritating. Kosei is even ignoring the directions on the sheet. The parts he should play quietly, and the parts he should play smoothly—all of them are breaking up and are disconnected.

No, no, this is all wrong. This isn't the "Moonlight Sonata." It's just noisy.

Stop...

This is wrong, stop!

Suddenly—he does. He puts his hands on his head and looks down. He looks like he's crying.

"No way..."

Takeshi's muttering, more like moaning, snaps me out of it. I've been in shock.

No...this isn't Kosei.

"It can't be!" I shout, and my whole body begins to tremble. What happened?

I can feel a chill running down my spine, little by little.

"Ahh!" Takeshi cries out loud and dashes out of the room.

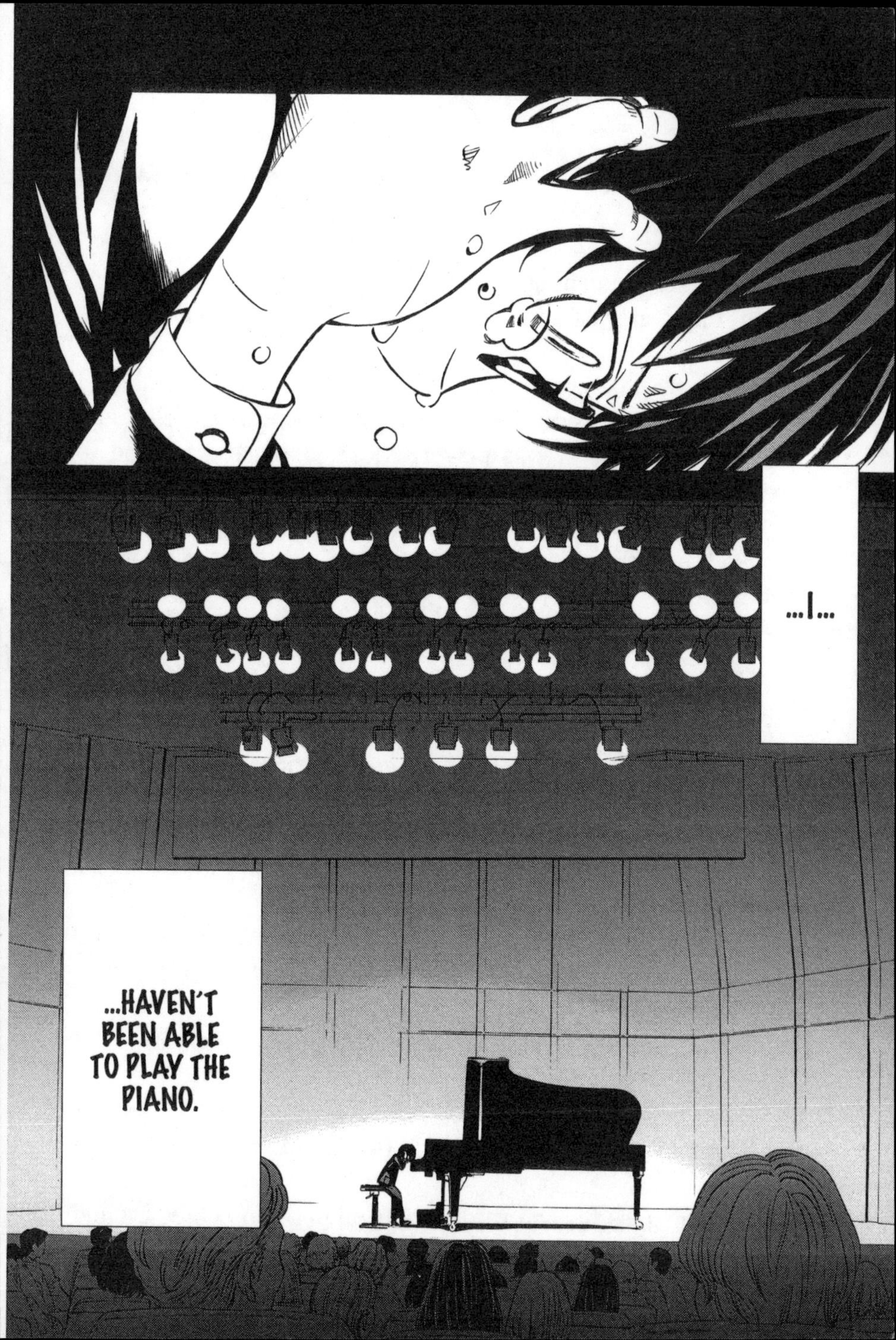
...I...
...HAVEN'T BEEN ABLE TO PLAY THE PIANO.

Miss Ochiai rushes in, almost getting run into by Takeshi at the door.

"Emi!"

I've been crouching down without even knowing. She helps me get up and walk and takes me to the waiting room.

I don't really remember what happened after that...how I played, I mean. It was like my mind was somewhere else, and I didn't know why I was playing there, or what I wanted to express with my "Fantaisie-Impromptu."

Kosei's name wasn't on the list of the final's winners.

At the very top was Takeshi's name, and mine was too, at the bottom.

Mine, when I'd played with no soul.

♪

Kosei doesn't show up to the next competition.

Or the next one.

Or the one after that.

I'm sure he'll come back. There's no way he can quit that easily.

Playing since you're little, every day, hour after hour, and having so much of your life taken up by piano, it becomes almost like breathing.

That's how it is for me. Kosei's gotta be the same way.

I wait intently for him to come back.

Takeshi and I wait and wait for Kosei. We're in middle school.

A year goes by, and the Maiho Competition comes around

again. I expect to see Kosei at last—ready to make his comeback, looking to pick up what he left behind, to erase his shame. But he doesn't show up.

This time at the Maiho Competition, as a first-year middle schooler, I barely make it through the first round. But Takeshi finishes in first place.

Every time I realized Kosei wasn't there, I got depressed and lost my motivation, but I guess Takeshi wasn't so obsessed with him.

Takeshi is standing in front of the list of players who passed the prelim and somehow looks frustrated by the results.

"Even when Kosei's not around, you push yourself hard, huh?" I ask him.

"I'm gonna keep on winning. I'll play perfectly, people will think my technique's great, and they'll keep comparing me to Kosei."

His words kind of hit me by surprise. Takeshi *is* obsessed with Kosei, just like me. Kosei is his reason for playing piano.

But then, where's Takeshi, himself, in all this?

Sure enough, the people looking at the results are saying:

—I wonder if Aiza's gonna be another Arima.

—Who'd have won if Arima were here, him or Aiza?

—Nah, I doubt Aiza would've been a match for Arima.

Even though they're talking about Takeshi, it's still Arima this and Arima that.

"Is that what you wanna hear?" I whisper. "Just Arima, Arima, Arima."

He grins. "As long as everybody's comparing us, they'll never forget Kosei. His perfect playing and his solid technique, I mean. That's why I'm gonna play like Kosei on purpose, so they keep comparing me to him, until the day he comes back."

Takeshi flashes me a thumbs up.

"I'm gonna keep his spot warm for him! That's a good idea, yeah, Emi? I mean, Igawa?"

"Come on, you're kidding me, right?"

"Huh?"

"Only you would ever come up with such an idea."

"R-Really?" he says, looking happy.

I turn and look straight at him. "I think you're right about keeping a spot for Kosei. I mean, our rivalry with him isn't over yet. He's gotta come back to exactly where he used to be."

"Right...we haven't caught up to him, and we haven't passed him. There's no way we can beat a guy who isn't here. Don't you think so, Em—uh..."

"Emi is fine."

Takeshi gives me a big nod, and I nod back at him.

"See you at the next round," Takeshi says and turns and leaves the hall, but as I watch him, tears fall from my eyes.

Being unable to play all winter, it really made me realize something. No matter what, I want to play piano. Piano's the only thing that lets me express everything I am. Piano's what I live for.

I play the way I do so people who hear me will never forget me.

I want to etch the memory of my piano into everyone's minds—a sound that can't be compared to anyone's, a sound all my own.

Is it different for Kosei?

Can he just walk away? Kosei, can you really just walk away from it?

I turn back to look at the results which don't have his name, glaring at them over people's heads.

Kosei etched his sound in my heart.

The way he played at the beginning—was it just a lie?

Kosei, why won't you show up? What did your piano mean to you?!

My bitter tears won't stop falling.

How could he carve his piano into my heart and then just act like a machine, and even leave?

How could he just betray me when, all this time, I kept on believing in the real Kosei from that first recital?

He wouldn't show me his real self and always lied to me. And just like that he disappeared.

"Kosei, you liar! You big fat liar!"

I stand still in the middle of the foyer and let my tears fall.

People pass me by in surprise, scrambling to avoid bumping into me, but I don't care—I just keep standing there. I don't even wipe my tears away.

Come back. Come back to me again, Kosei, you liar.

Even if you're still a liar. Just come back...

♯ 3 ⟦ ♪ Kosei, You're Too Kind ⟧ Tsubaki Sawabe

It happened four and a half years ago...at the beginning of winter in my fourth year of elementary school. A cold rain was falling that day.

I, Tsubaki Sawabe, was running around in the rain, looking for Chelsea with Kosei Arima.

Chelsea is the Arimas' pet cat. They live next door.

She's jet-black, and I don't think she was fully grown back then.

Kosei and I had been playing on the grounds of a shrine about half a year earlier when we found her. She'd been put in a cardboard box and abandoned in the space under the main building.

♪   ♪   ♪

After school, a summer day when we were in fourth grade.

The shrine was unattended, and I was playing on the grounds, practicing my swing and bouncing a ball against the wall. Before going out to play I'd asked Kosei to come along, but he'd told me, *Nope, I gotta practice my piano.* And yet all of a sudden, there he was at the shrine.

"Finished your lesson? Okay, wanna play catch?" I asked him, delighted that he'd come.

He pushed up his black-rimmed glasses and gave me a vague smile. "Well, my mom seemed tired, so I'm having a little break. She asked me to go buy something, but I thought maybe I'd stop by here and pray."

"You mean to win at your piano competition?"

Kosei shook his head. "No, winning or losing is just the result. I want to pray that I don't get nervous and that my practice pays off...and..."

His head sank.

"What's wrong?"

"Uhh...nothing."

Kosei faced the worship hall, clapped twice, and then closed his eyes, deep in prayer.

At the time, I didn't know that Kosei's mom—Mrs. Saki Arima—had gotten so sick that except for Kosei's piano lessons, she had to spend a lot of time lying down and couldn't take care of things around the house. A few months later, his mom started going in and out of the hospital, and about a year after that, she ended up being hospitalized for good.

I'm sure that what Kosei was praying for then was for his mom to get better.

"Well, since you came all the way here, Kosei, let's play. Even just a little."

He hesitated a few seconds about it and then agreed.

"Well...okay, for a little while."

He threw the rubber ball, and I hit it with my plastic bat, and he went to catch it.

After a few times of that, I hit the ball a little too far, and it rolled under the empty main hall.

Kosei went after it. He knelt on the stone pavement and peered into the space and grew still.

"What's wrong? Is it too deep for you to reach?"

When I moved closer, Kosei looked back at me, put a finger to his lips, and said, "Shhh. Don't you hear a sound coming from that box?"

Under the building was a really old, tiny cardboard box, and the ball had stopped right next to it. It seemed like the ball had hit the box. The lid was closed with a piece of adhesive tape that lightly held together just one spot at the middle of the seam.

I squatted down and pricked up my ears.

A scratching sound came from inside the box.

"What's that?" I whispered.

Kosei reached out his hand like he'd made up his mind. "Let's open it up and see. It's gotta be an animal. It can't get out from the box."

Kosei might seem timid, but in fact he's pretty curious, and he's just too kind to look the other way.

"Wha—are you serious? Okay, but you don't wanna get bitten...lemme do it."

Kosei needs his hands for piano. If I let anything happen to them, his mom would let me have it—heck, she might kill me. I pushed him aside and pulled the box out.

Meow...meow.

A tiny voice spilled out from the gap in the lid, and we

looked at each other.

"A cat!"

We ripped off the tape and opened the lid, and this jet-black cat was all crouched up like it was afraid. It wasn't small enough to be a newborn, but nor was it big enough to be an adult.

"So cute," Kosei said before I could make a sound. "Tsubaki, this cat must've been abandoned. Put here so it couldn't break out of the box and get back home."

"What an awful thing to do!" I got mad, but Kosei just kept gazing at the black kitten.

"I'm gonna bring it home with me."

"For real?"

I was shocked. I didn't think Kosei's super-scary mom would ever allow it. She got angry when he played with *me*. But if he didn't get out and have fun, his eyes got dull and gray and his face turned pale, so we always played in secret. I didn't budge an inch on that point. We played secretly so we wouldn't get caught.

"I think it'd be better for us to raise it here, together. Bring it food," I suggested. "If it'd be tough for the two of us, we could rope Ryota or somebody into helping."

Ryota Watari, a classmate of ours, was the leader of a bunch of clowns but wasn't a bad kid.

"If an adult finds it, though, it'll get taken to a shelter for sure."

Saying this, Kosei stroked the cat's back gingerly. The cat just trembled, looking like it didn't even have the energy to resist.

"It must be hungry," I noted. "It probably hasn't even had any water despite this terrible muggy weather. 'Cause there's nothing else in the box."

I rushed over to the hand-washing basin several dozen feet away, scooped some water with my hands, and put them close to the cat's mouth when I returned.

The cat sniffed before lapping up the water frantically.

Kosei's face lit up, and he ran to get some water, too. We couldn't carry very much since it dripped through our fingers, but we took turns ferrying water to the cat.

Meoww...mee-oww.

The cat didn't seem scared of humans and purred and rubbed its face against our hands. Clearly relieved, it lay down and nodded off. Every time it breathed, its belly went up and down, and it felt warm.

It was alive.

"Yeah, I'm bringing it home with me. End of story." Kosei picked up the box with the cat still inside.

"Are you sure about this? Your mom's gonna explode."

"I'm sure." Behind Kosei's black-rimmed glasses, his eyes twinkled. "I'm gonna ask as nice as I can if I can keep her. Mom likes animals, too. When I was little she always used to tell me about how she had cats when she was a kid. She had three of them, actually."

Kosei started walking as he spoke.

"I'm sure it will be fine," he whispered to the cat inside the box.

I tagged along with him, hoping we could beg his mom together. But Kosei said no.

"I'll ask her alone. So just wait, Tsubaki, and don't worry."

I made up my mind that if it didn't work, I'd ask my parents instead. There I stayed, waiting outside Kosei's house the whole time, not going inside my own home next door.

The sun of the long summer day started to set, and evening

came.

"Tsubaki, are you out there? Dinner's ready," my mom called, but I kept on waiting. Then, when the sky had turned a dark violet, Kosei finally peeped out from the entryway door.

"How'd it go?" I asked excitedly.

Kosei answered in no rush. "Ah, I was waiting for you, but it didn't look like you were in your room...so I was coming to tell you."

You can get a clear view into my home from the windows in Kosei's house, and vice versa.

"Well? Come on, how'd it go?" I asked again. Actually, I didn't need to. I could tell from his sunny expression.

"I can keep it!" he answered happily. "Well, if my dad says so...but dad's never told mom no, not even once."

"Nice! So, what do we call it?"

Kosei took a piece of candy with the wrapping paper all wrinkled out of his jeans pocket. He put it on his palm and showed it to me.

"While I was begging my mom, I guess the cat was hungry, 'cause she got out of the box, hopped on the table, and licked my candy." Beaming, Kosei told me, "So it's Chelsea. After the candy."

♪ ♪ ♪

Half a year passed.

I often visited Kosei's house next door, wanting to see Chelsea. For some reason they wouldn't let me in the house, but Kosei would show up holding Chelsea so I could play with her in the entryway.

He'd leave Chelsea with me and go right back inside and

start practicing on the piano. He played the same sounds over and over, again and again...

On a day off from school, when a cold winter rain was falling, I visited Kosei as usual and asked him to let me play with Chelsea.

Usually he would show up right away, taking a quick break from his piano practice, but that day was different. There was a pause, and then his mom showed up.

Now that I think about it, his mom had mostly stopped showing herself to me, and whenever she did, she looked more haggard and skinnier, but I didn't notice at the time.

"Tsubaki, I'm sorry... Chelsea is gone. Maybe she didn't like this house..."

I can't remember what her face looked like when she said that to me. I was just so shocked that I announced right away, "Wow, I gotta find Chelsea!"

I was about to run outside, but Kosei came bounding out. Although my memory's a little fuzzy, I think his eyes were swollen from crying a lot.

"*I'll* find Chelsea!"

He almost pushed me away, grabbed his raincoat, and ran out into the rain with his shoes halfway on.

"Kosei!" I remember clearly how his mom raised her voice almost like she was screaming. "No!! What about practice?!"

Then she crumpled, falling to her knees.

"Please don't go, Kosei... Don't go looking for her... Forgive me."

I couldn't stand seeing her like that with her head hanging.

"I-I'm gonna look for Chelsea and Kosei."

I almost felt like I was flung out, umbrella in hand. I put it up and looked to the right and the left of the street trying to find Kosei through the rain, but he was nowhere to be seen.

Quickly trying to remember the places he might go, I ran down the school route, calling out for Kosei and Chelsea.

I went to the shrine where we found Chelsea, but no Kosei.

"He isn't taking shelter... Maybe he went back home."

My clothes were wet from the windy rain, and I was very cold.

I went back to my house and changed out of my wet clothes. From the closet, I took out a sketchbook that I had left over from preschool and made some flyers for a lost cat.

I drew a cat painted all black with a black magic marker.

—Missing. Name: Chelsea. Color: Black. Eyes: Gold. Female. Wearing red collar.

"Done!"

Okay, now I just needed them to let me put these flyers on the community bulletin board in the park, in convenience stores, in supermarkets, and at businesses that my friends' parents ran.

That's when I noticed how quiet it seemed. I thought it was because of the rain...but even when I listened carefully, I couldn't hear Kosei's piano, which always came faintly from his house next door.

"Kosei's not home yet? He's still looking for her?"

Then I gotta look for Chelsea, too. I won't give up till I find her. I'm gonna come back with Kosei and Chelsea.

When I stepped out from my house, the cold air soaked into my body. On top of that, the rain was pouring harder than before.

I went back inside, placed the flyers in a plastic bag to keep them from getting wet, and also put some scotch tape in my pocket, after nearly forgetting it.

"Let's do this!"

I put up my umbrella resolutely and ran out into the street in the rain.

"Kosei! Chelsea!"

I ran all over calling their names. I went to the school route again, around the school, the riverbed where we often played together, our old preschool, the children's playground in the residential area, the shopping arcade...

On the way, I stopped at two supermarkets and three convenience stores, the dental clinic run by my friend's parents, and a beauty salon I knew, and asked them to let me put up the flyers.

Once the rain let up a bit, I'd ask the man in charge of our community center who always came by to hand out notices to let me post my two remaining flyers on the board in the children's playground. If they weren't enough, I'd make more.

"Kosei! Chelsea!"

No matter where I looked, and no matter whom I asked when I put up the flyers, I couldn't find Kosei.

"You must've stopped somewhere to get out of the rain, didn't you? Or did you go home already?"

'Cause it's so cold outside.

My resolve was wilting from the terrible weather, and it was getting darker, so I decided to go home. None of the lights were on in Kosei's house. I wondered if his mom was out looking for him, too.

"Oh, no. He must still be out there. I can't stay home, I gotta go."

My mom was worried about me, but I convinced her to let me go out for a third time.

The rain was already so bad that the umbrella wasn't much

use anymore. As I shivered, I tried to come up with places where you might avoid the rain. I decided to go to the shrine again.

Kosei wasn't there.

My heart ached. It was hard to breathe. Even my stomach was hurting from not being able to find Kosei. It was getting darker and darker. The streetlights flicked on above me as I trudged along the sidewalk.

"Where are you..."

Then I remembered the big park far away that we'd only gone to twice.

"No way...that far? That's in the next school district..."

We were the only ones who knew about the place, having trekked there to adventure in other kids' territory.

"If I go there...it'll be totally dark by the time I get back home."

They'll be so worried, my mom and Kosei's mom, too. I'm gonna get a real scolding.

But Kosei and I were scolded all the time, anyway. If I told his mom that I'd dragged him around looking for Chelsea, maybe she wouldn't scold him so much. Less than me, at least.

I headed over there.

♪

On the way to that distant place, I found Kosei in the small children's park near Ryota's house.

I was freezing, so I wanted to get something to drink to get warm. I walked up to a vending machine on the sidewalk opposite from the park entrance and was getting some coins from the wallet in my pocket when it happened.

I dropped a one-hundred-yen coin. I bent down to pick it up and happened to look straight ahead. Underneath a park slide shaped like a piggy, in the tunnel in the body, sat a figure with his arms around his knees.

"Hey, Kosei?"

I hurried and bought a can of hot lemonade. It was what he'd bought for me the other day when I was a little sick with a cold.

"You're not a gorilla."

That's what he told me when Ryota and some other boys teased me saying even a "female gorilla" caught colds. Kosei treated me to the can of lemonade and a gentle smile from behind those black-rimmed glasses.

"You're a girl."

I'd felt a lump in my throat, for the first time in my life. I'd also tasted a can of hot lemonade for the first time in my life—its sourness, its sweetness, and its warmth. It's a taste I'll never forget.

I stared at the figure again, my eyes wide open in the gloom. I was sure that was Kosei with the raincoat on.

Whew. There you are.

Holding the hot can with two fingers, I crossed the street and ran over to the tunnel under the piggy slide.

For some reason, I almost started to cry. It was really cold, and I was shivering. My legs were shaking.

"Kosei!"

I called him as I peeked into the tunnel, and he glanced at me, looking surprised for a moment. From all the rain his shoes were wet, his legs were wet, his hands were wet, and his bangs were wet, and so was his face, too. His eyes were red, and I could tell he'd been crying.

"I knew it, I knew you were here."

No, I couldn't have. But I knew I'd never stop looking, no matter how far I had to go.

"Tsubaki..."

"I made flyers for Chelsea. And I put up a lot of them, at shops and stuff."

I pointed out the plastic bag that I'd put in my umbrella on the ground. Kosei shook his head hard like when a little baby doesn't like something.

"Huh? What's wrong?" I asked him, but he kept silent, biting his lip and holding his knees.

Then I noticed that he had a bandage wrapped around his left hand. The bandage was wet and dirty and plastered with dead leaves from the enkianthus shrubbery in the park. He must've stuck in his hands all over the place to look for Chelsea.

Wait a minute... Had he hurt his hand badly enough to need a bandage? Ouch. He couldn't play piano...

"What happened to your hand?"

"It was...my fault." Kosei put his right hand onto his left. "I was minding her too much... Chelsea scratched me...and it bled a lot."

"Chelsea did?"

"It was my fault, not hers!"

I wasn't sure what really happened, but it seemed like Chelsea had caused his wound. Then Kosei burst into tears.

"Chelsea... I'm sorry, Chelsea!"

"Okay...right."

I didn't know how to continue after that. If I said it wasn't his fault, then it would be Chelsea's, but I wasn't gonna tell him it was his fault when he was suffering and crying.

"Drink it."

I went into the tunnel and gave the hot lemonade to Kosei, who was crying so hard his nose was running.

"It's getting dark, so let's go home, yeah? You gotta dry yourself or you'll catch a cold."

Kosei sniffed his runny nose and started speaking in a choked voice.

"Chelsea was nowhere. Even in the dumpsite or under the bridge. It's so cold outside, she'll die if she's out here."

A teardrop fell—and then another—onto the bandage wrapped around his hand as he continued to hold his knees.

"I couldn't say anything...even though I knew my mom was going out to dump her."

Dump her—

I realized that Kosei's mom had lied to me.

I was so shocked.

He kept talking while I was in shock.

"If I'd complained, Chelsea might still be alive...but I couldn't say anything. I-I couldn't say anything to my mom."

Kosei let out a loud sob and held himself tight. His body was shaking violently.

"They're right. I'm a doll with no heart that my mom made!"

Why would Kosei ever think that he had no heart? But he must have been told that by somebody...by many people, since he said "they."

How terrible, who's been telling him such things?!

For all the anger I felt, I didn't even know who they were.

I couldn't help being angry, though, and couldn't forgive them.

Kosei was crying, his face buried in his knees, and I had no words for him. I felt so bitter and sad that it felt like my heart was being torn apart.

I actually didn't see him cry often. Most of the time he was smiling, and he rarely got angry.

I can't abandon Kosei when he's crying so sadly. When it pains me so much. No one should shed tears like those.

I moved forward with my knees on the sandy, rough concrete.

"No, Kosei. You have a heart. There are so many great things about you. I know that. Like..."

Umm, what? When it comes to counting them...there're just too many, or maybe too few? He's always himself, and smiling, and it's hard to tell what he's thinking most of the time.

But he never lied.

He was always thinking about others. He was so kind and caring.

He was never selfish.

"Uh...okay, see? You were running around so hard. That's because you regret what happened, right? 'Cause you wanna say sorry to Chelsea?"

His face was still buried, and he kept on crying.

If you had no heart, you wouldn't feel sad or bitter or cry from regret. Not a chance.

"You've got heart, Kosei, for sure."

He just wasn't good at expressing himself. He smiled a lot instead.

He held back when he might say things.

"It's just that you've become too good at hiding your feelings—so good even you can't find them."

Kosei's skinny shoulders twitched.

My heart was breaking and in pain... I wanted so badly to see his usual peaceful smile.

"So I'll find them for you. That way, you won't get lost or

have regrets... I'll always be by your side."

I sat next to him.

"I know everything about you, okay?"

I really thought so then.

♪

Having learned that Chelsea hadn't run away but had been left somewhere too far away, I went around taking the flyers back, lying that we'd found her.

I'd never told such a painful lie and had to look down the whole time 'cause I thought my expression would give me away.

One day a while later, Kosei was standing in his backyard, spaced out in a sunny spot in the winter sun. I was home and saw his head behind the low hedge, so I went out and spoke to him from the alley.

"Hey, Kosei, what're you doing?"

Looking surprised, he hid something behind his back and said, "Oh, nothing. I'm gonna go out for a bit. I'll be okay by myself."

Strange. He was acting odd.

"Sure. See you around."

With that, I snuck behind my house's door. I took a moment and then looked outside. Kosei was headed for the dumpsite alone, a garbage bag for non-burnable trash in one hand.

It was obvious what was in it 'cause the garbage bag was transparent.

The red collar, the food bowl that Kosei had written Chelsea's name on, and the cat toilet...

"Hey, wait!"

I got so angry, I ran out and grabbed the garbage bag.

"This... You're doing this alone? That means Chelsea's never coming back..."

Kosei avoided eye contact, looking remorseful. "I just thought you'd be sad...if you saw."

"Don't worry about me! Did you give up already?!"

"There's nothing...I can do..."

He contorted his face trying to smile...his eyes brimming with tears.

"It's...my—"

"It's not your fault!"

Angry and sad, I snatched the garbage bag from Kosei's hand.

"You shouldn't be going by yourself. You shouldn't have to do such a sad thing all on your own. I said I'll always be with you, didn't I? When you're hurting, I'll be with you, so just tell me. If you haven't given up, then tell me!"

"I don't wanna throw them away... But if I don't...I get distracted. I'm always looking at them."

"Did your mom say that?"

Kosei gave a small nod. "Then she should put the toilet and bowl away somewhere instead of keeping them in the piano room... But she can't even do that. So I have to act sorry and put them away. 'Cause I know she regrets it, even if she doesn't say so."

"...Kosei, you're too kind."

I couldn't say anything more.

Something hot welled up in my throat instead.

He smiled like he was about to cry. "See? I knew you were gonna be sad, Tsubaki. That's why I wanted to go and throw them away by myself."

"No...it's not right for you to keep doing these things alone.

I said I'd stay with you. I...don't cry. I'm strong."

I held back my tears. See? I wasn't crying.

"Well," he said in a little bit of distress, "when I told you the truth, that Chelsea was dumped, you looked so sad... Afterwards, I thought you were hurt worse than me."

Dummy...

I couldn't answer him—and just held the garbage bag to my chest.

"I'm gonna keep this for you," I finally managed. "You'll need them when we find Chelsea someday."

When I turned away, Kosei let out a relieved mutter.

"Thanks, Tsubaki."

I ran inside my house...and wept silently.

Why does Kosei have to be so kind?

♪   ♪   ♪

The other thing happened...about three years ago. It was autumn and we were in sixth grade.

Kosei's mom—Mrs. Saki Arima's illness had gotten worse. She had passed away at the beginning of summer vacation that year, and this was right after the forty-ninth-day memorial.

Kosei was sitting at the piano and practicing, like always. My mom heard him playing and asked me to go see how he was doing.

I would have anyway. If he was playing more harshly than usual, or if it was the opposite and he couldn't really practice, I'd know he was upset.

But Kosei hadn't changed at all. He was practicing at an indifferent pace, at exactly the same time and in exactly the same way he'd been practicing for years.

The way he was behaving, I couldn't help feeling worried about him.

I sneaked in through a window, and then into his piano room.

He didn't seem to notice me and kept playing the whole time. He made the same sound over and over, sometimes tapping the keys strongly, sometimes tapping them softly.

I was there in the corner when Kosei suddenly spoke without even turning around.

"Tsubaki, you see that stuffed animal?"

He'd known the whole time.

"My dad found it when he was cleaning mom's room. It's a cat...isn't it?"

There was a white thing lying on the floor next to a chair. I picked it up and saw it was a handmade stuffed animal. It wasn't well made at all, and the face was drawn with a black magic marker.

"I think it was supposed to be Chelsea. My mom might've made it for me in secret. I didn't know."

"Well, this is white."

"But I'm sure it's Chelsea."

I remembered Chelsea's collar and the bowl that Kosei's mom couldn't throw away, and it made my heart ache. I hugged the clumsy-looking stuffed animal. Then I put my back against Kosei's—his piano seat didn't have a backrest—and leaned on him lightly.

I could feel the warmth of his body and the movement of his back muscles.

Without saying a word, he kept playing.

"Kosei..."

"Yes?"

"Are you gonna play in the Maiho Competition final?"

The final. It was happening next Sunday, probably.

"Yeah, I ought to since I passed the prelim." His hands stopped, and neither stammering nor trying to sound brave, he went on plainly. "I'm terrible, aren't I? My mom just died. But I'm more worried about the competition that's coming up. I really am a bad person..."

"Are you okay?"

"I'm okay. That's just the way I was made."

After that he said something like he was fine because he practiced a lot...but I was scared to ask more. I had a bad feeling.

Yeah, something's wrong.

No way he's not upset.

He hasn't vented to anybody, anywhere.

The kinds of empty condolences that the moms in our neighborhood were offering him—"I know it's hard, but if you cheer up and do your best, it'd make your mom happy in heaven"—nauseated me.

I happened to catch the same ladies talking about him behind his back—about how they thought it was creepy that he didn't even cry.

So...I didn't know what to say to him.

But I promised. To stay with him. I'll be right by his side.

Holding the cat doll to my chest, I kept quiet and stayed there with him.

Having said his bit, Kosei, too, went back to playing again. The piece was intense.

That day, the clouds flowed swiftly and blocked, now and then, the sunshine coming in through the window.

A few days later, the final round of the Maiho Competition was held in central Tokyo.

I went to the competition to hear Kosei play.

I sat in the back of the first floor in the hall.

As one kid after another came on stage, I listened to the announcements about who was playing. I couldn't tell how far along we were in the program just from hearing the pieces. I waited and waited for Kosei's turn.

People started whispering when it arrived, and it made me sad. 'Cause they didn't sound like they were welcoming him or expecting anything from his performance.

I guess Kosei had won so many times he'd become a heel.

At last he showed up on the lit stage.

He was gonna play Beethoven. He bowed and started to play, not looking especially nervous or excited—there was no expression on his face.

Kosei always practiced in small bits, but listening to the song all the way through from the beginning now, the melody was so much more intense, and his momentum and speed made it seem like he was banging the keys... It was when the piece shifted into this beautifully flowing tune that people around me started acting weird.

Like everybody was tense, or appalled, or astonished, or angry...

They couldn't talk since the performance was still going on, but this strange mood was swallowing up the hall.

And then, on stage, Kosei suddenly stopped playing and cradled his head.

Is he crying?
...Kosei's crying!!

The audience started murmuring, and a staff person showed

up and took Kosei to the wing, pushing his back.

What happened?! Kosei, are you all right??

He'd been upset, after all. So deep inside him that he didn't even know—but I'd noticed.

Now it had burst out all at once at the most important time.

Kosei! You shouldn't be alone!

I really believed that, without any basis.

I had no idea what I could do for him, but I absolutely wanted to keep my promise to stay with him.

You have to keep promises. Maybe I can't do a thing, but I can shut up and remain by his side and put my hand on his shoulder until he stops crying. That much I can do. I want to do it!

I rushed backstage.

But Kosei wasn't there. I didn't even know the place but ran around looking for him...

"There you are, Kosei!"

His face was all pale, and he didn't even try to wipe his tears, he just let them spill. A woman I recognized took him out the back entrance in a hurry. She'd been in and out of Kosei's house more often since his mom was hospitalized. This time I only saw her profile for a moment.

"Kosei!"

I called out to him, but he didn't turn around. He disappeared behind the door of a car. I chased after them as fast as I could, but of course I couldn't catch up to a car that was driving away... I couldn't stay with him after all.

♪

I didn't know when he'd gone back home after that... His house stayed dark. But about three days later, Kosei came to school. He might've been staying at some other house.

"Morning, Kosei. We got these printouts in class while you were gone. And you should copy the homework now."

I'd waited for him at the classroom entrance, and jumped out into the hallway and held the sheets and my notebook out to him. Kosei lifted his head slowly and let out, "Oh, okay..."

He borrowed my notebook and copied the homework, gave it back to me right away, and thanked me with a blank expression.

"Hey, Kosei. Do you wanna play dodgeball during lunch break? You just have to avoid getting hit. You don't need to touch the ball. We gotta get everybody together and dash over to the gym or else the fifth graders are gonna take it. They come really early these days."

"...Mm."

He was absentminded the whole time, and when I talked to him, he hardly reacted or even glanced at me. But he didn't look too depressed. He finished his lunch without leaving anything, either.

The next day, or maybe the day after that...I started noticing that the bathroom light in Kosei's house was sometimes on, in addition to the light in his room upstairs.

"Oh, Kosei's home."

But not a single note came from the piano. The light in the music room was never on, either.

A few days passed, but it was still the same.

Kosei...did you quit playing piano?

But as soon as the thought popped into my head, I turned it down. That wasn't it.

It's because he'd cry if he played. It's hard on him.

I remembered vividly how Kosei was on stage—sitting there with the piano in front of him under the blinding bright light, holding his head in his hands and crying.

But there are some things that you can't let go of unless you cry and shout them out. Kosei looked like he was scared of doing that.

How might I soothe the uneasiness and sadness that he'd locked away in his heart? No matter how cheerfully I talked to him and invited him to do this or that, it was no use.

I didn't care if he told me I was annoying.

I just talked about fun things when I was with him.

I stayed with him all the time. Even after we went home, I gazed at his house from my window all the time.

Kosei's expression slowly went back to how it used to be, and around the beginning of the winter, he started smiling gently when he looked at me, so on the surface it seemed like he'd calmed down.

If I went to his house in the morning, he'd walk to school with me, and we'd have our usual conversations. It wasn't like he wore the same old dirty clothes or never washed his face.

Kosei was back.

But...not his piano.

No matter how much time passed, I didn't hear one note.

I thought maybe his hand hurt, and since we were in the same group in science class, I watched him carefully during our experiment, but it didn't seem like that was it. In gym class, he didn't look like he was minding his hand, either. And in home ec, he used a knife and a frying pan during cooking practice.

Before, he'd always been careful about not hurting his hands.

He's still not himself. He isn't the real Kosei without his piano. But...maybe playing still makes him sad and makes him cry, and it hurts him to cry.

"Did you quit piano?"

I came out and asked Kosei this, just once. He gave me a vague smile and shook his head.

Right after that, though, I saw him standing in front of the piano after music class, our sixth period. When I noticed, my feet halted by the back door, and I watched over him, holding my breath.

He didn't leave even though it would be cleaning time soon.

The lid of the piano was open, and he touched one of the white keys around the center timidly with his right middle finger. *Duum*, he tapped it, making a single sound.

And he had such a complex look on his face...like he was relieved or something. Then he ran out of the room. I hurried after him but got stopped by one of my friends, so I didn't get a chance to talk to him.

Kosei...I guess you still want to play piano?

But still no note came from his house.

His place was always quiet and there were no lights on in the living room or the kitchen, so I couldn't even tell if anyone was home.

I wondered what he was doing, keeping so quiet in a dark house... I was worried, but it'd be rude to be watching all the time. Glancing in from my window now and then was the most I could do.

And then winter came.

Christmas evening—

While my mom and I waited for my dad to come home with warm fried chicken, we prepared for our home party. Having ordered some Bûche de Noël—a chocolate cake shaped like a log—from a pastry shop, we put it in the center of the dining table along with some glasses and a fizzy, bottled drink.

In the living room was a three-foot Christmas tree—a fake—that we'd decorated with ornaments. It was very warm inside the house. Outside, though, the first cold wave of the winter was setting in.

"Why is dad taking so long? I'm hungry."

"He'll be home soon. He texted saying he got to the station. I'll bet the fried chicken shop was crowded," my mom said, checking the taste of the pot-au-feu.

I opened the curtain and looked out through the window.

Kosei's home was totally dark.

Of course, it's Christmas. Kosei must be at somebody's house having a party. He didn't look so sad when we were coming home from school.

That's what I was thinking when I saw something move in the dark window of his house.

Wh-What? A robber??

I hurried and told my mom. We watched together quietly from behind the curtain.

"...It's hard to tell."

Then my dad came home.

"I'm ho-ome. You said to get the large box of chicken, right?"

For a second I thought it should've been medium 'cause there were only three of us, but we quickly hushed him up— the chicken could wait.

"Next door, the Arimas' house. It looks like they're out,

but did you notice anything strange?"

"No, why? Did something happen?" my dad asked with a blank look.

"Dad, could you go check?"

"What?? Me? By myself?"

Eventually, we geared up—I got a bat, dad took out a golf club, and mom had the broom we used for cleaning the entrance. Shining a flashlight, with dad in the front but huddled close together, we inched along our own wall. We lit the window of the Arimas' over the low fencing between our houses.

The white face that appeared behind the pane looked surprised by the beam of light.

"Whoa!"

It was my dad who screamed.

"Kosei?!" I asked.

"What? Is it you, Ko??"

My mom noticed too after I shouted out his name. It was Kosei with a blanket over his head in the dark. He was staring our way.

"You've been home by yourself? What're you doing? Let us in!"

My mom and I rushed to the Arimas' entrance, and waiting impatiently for Kosei to unlock the door, we barged in.

It was very cold in the house. The heater didn't seem to be on. I had to grope around in total darkness to find the light switches for the entryway and the hall.

We prodded Kosei, who still had the blanket on, and proceeded, turning on all the lights on the first floor. The place wasn't exactly a mess, but some bags of burnable garbage were piled up near the backdoor in the kitchen. The see-through bags were full of empty bento boxes from convenience stores and packages from other ready-made meals.

Most of it was sandwich wrappers. There were seals on them that had the logo of a bakery in the shopping arcade. All the labels said "Egg Sandwich."

Egg sandwiches...Kosei's favorite. It got me thinking that maybe the bento boxes were what his dad had eaten, while Kosei had just been eating sandwiches.

"Oh, Ko... Why? And with the lights and heater off."

My mom hugged Kosei like she was jumping him and sounded like she was gonna cry. He murmured his reply like he didn't know what to say.

"I get scared when it's bright... 'Cause I can tell that no one's here..."

"Isn't it scarier in the dark?" my mom asked.

At this, Kosei fell silent and bit his lip. Watching from behind my mom, somehow I felt like I understood.

It's more painful than scary—to see things as they are.

His house had been dark the whole time.

He'd been home alone the whole time.

"You must be freezing, Ko."

"Yeah...but I'm okay. It's just me here anyway."

"What are you talking about? Of course you're not okay. You're gonna catch a cold. It's Christmas, let's go to our house and have dinner together. Right, Tsubaki?"

Mom was right. I was almost crying, too.

Being alone in a cold house with no lights on for Christmas...

"Yeah, good idea. My dad went and bought too much chicken, so you gotta help us finish it."

Stupid Kosei. You were even gazing longingly at our bright dining room. Why are you doing this to yourself? I told you so many times I'd be with you and to let me know when you're hurting. Why can't you be honest and rely on me? Why are you always worrying about bothering other people?

My mom and I dragged him over to our house—the Sawabe residence.

First, we put him in the dining room, and my mom spoke to my dad in a low voice out in the hallway.

"Is Takahiko on another business trip? He could've just asked us to take care of Ko. Sometimes there's a note in our mailbox saying he'll be gone for a few days so would we please look after his son. Why didn't he let us know on such a cold day? Did I do anything to make him feel like I expected something in return?"

I heard that Mr. Arima—Kosei's father had to go out of town a lot for his job.

My mom would worry and invite Kosei over, but Kosei always refused like he'd be bothering us.

"Ah," my dad said, "when I went out to get the paper this morning, I think I saw a note or something on top, but when I took the stuff out of the mailbox, the wind blew it away."

"That was it! Pay attention."

When we went back into the dining room, Kosei was sitting on a chair and looking warm and relaxed, which relaxed us, too. His pale cheeks were turning pink. His lips were getting their color back as well.

"Kosei, do you want some pot-au-feu? It'll warm you up."

I put some into a stew bowl from the pot. I went a little heavy on the sausages. This wasn't lunch duty at school, so no one would tease me or complain.

"Is this..."

Kosei looked a little surprised.

"That's right, Ko. You remember the smell, don't you? Your mom gave me the recipe. I think that was around when you entered preschool. There was such a delicious smell coming from your kitchen, I had to ask your mom to share her secret family recipe."

That was news to me.

So it was Kosei's mom's recipe.

He must've thought he'd never be able to taste his mom's cooking again.

It made me excited to think how happy he'd feel. I finished serving everybody's bowl and placed some side dishes on the table. Then I put the chicken on a big plate, too. My mom cut up the log cake.

"Ko, you can have the big one."

"No, that's mine!"

"I'm okay with a small one, Mrs. Sawabe."

"C'mon, Tsubaki, don't be so greedy."

"Whaaat. Fine, Kosei's like my little brother."

All festive, we sat down around the table.

My dad popped the fizzy drink. It made a loud sound, and the cork hit the ceiling, landed between Kosei and me as we covered our ears, hit the corner of the table, and bounced onto the floor.

"Merry Christmas!" we toasted.

Kosei bashfully clinked his glass with mine.

I watched him as I ate my cake, hoping to see him love the pot-au-feu. Kosei ate his cake and the chicken my dad offered him but didn't make a move for the bowl.

"The pot-au-feu's really good," I said, scooping some of the soup, jam-packed with the rich flavor of vegetables, and bringing it to my mouth, just to make Kosei try it too. "It was stewing for half a day. I helped make it—well, I peeled the onions. Mom used celery in the bouquet garni to make the stock, but you eat celery, right?"

"What's wrong, Ko? Don't be shy," my mom urged.

"Okay..."

Kosei seemed to stifle a sigh. Finally he scooped some and tasted it.

He frowned, like he was in pain, but in the end he gulped it down. When he brought another bite up to his lips, he turned pale.

He dropped his spoon, covered his mouth with his hand, and ran out of the room.

"Kosei?!" I yelled.

"Ko!"

"Poor Kosei..."

We ran after him, but he darted into the bathroom...and didn't come out for a long time.

"W-We did something awful to Ko. We were forcing kindness on him," my mom muttered very sadly.

My dad looked really serious, too. "It hurts him to remember his mother...not being able to get back what he lost. His mom's cooking, the piano, all of it, is just too much for him to take. Bright rooms, welcoming homes, happy families, all of it."

"Kosei... This sucks. Is there nothing I can do? Mom, dad." I couldn't help clinging to my parents and shaking them. "It's not enough just staying with him, I gotta do something. Something..." There was no way I could leave Kosei as he was. "He doesn't want what people should want most, like warmth, tasty stuff, and bright places? Is he never going to be able to accept any happiness? It's not right."

Maybe he couldn't stand up on his own. It wasn't enough

just to watch over him. I had to reach out and pull him up, to help him get up.

"I thought so too," my mom said. "But...if it's counterproductive, maybe just looking over him would be best. If it's just self-satisfaction, it's unfair to him."

"It isn't self-satisfaction!"

But mom and dad got more and more lost in thought. We all went quiet and hung our heads for a while.

What do I do?

About half an hour passed. Kosei didn't come out no matter how long we waited. No sound came from the bathroom, even when we stood close.

"This isn't good... He didn't pass out, did he?" my dad said.

Warning that he was opening the door, he turned the knob. It wasn't locked, maybe because Kosei had been in such a hurry.

As expected, Kosei had passed out—on the lid of the toilet after closing it.

"Kosei!"

He looked so pale, and the area around his mouth was a little dirty. He'd thrown up. His glasses and handkerchief were on the floor.

"Oh, no. Call an ambulance!"

At my mom's loud voice, Kosei opened his eyes.

"I'm sorry... I think I fell asleep. I can't sleep well at home... I guess this house feels comfy..."

He tried to stand up but staggered. He groped to find his glasses, so I handed them to him.

"Kosei, stay overnight. Here, rinse your mouth."

I took him to the washbasin, filled a glass with warm water, and gave it to him. He rinsed his mouth and washed his hands... but then said, "I can't anymore," like he was gonna fall asleep right there.

"Oh, geez."

"I'll carry him," my dad said, but I told him no. My chest felt tight as I lent a shoulder to Kosei, who was barely awake, but I took him to the guest room, where my mom laid a futon.

He's a boy, so how come he's so thin and light? He hasn't been eating well, I bet that's why. He must only be eating egg sandwiches, apart from lunch at school since our class goal is zero leftovers. Dummy. Take better care of yourself.

I even started feeling angry.

He's doomed at this rate. He's gotta eat more, at least. If he doesn't, where'll he find his energy?

I made up my mind.

I'd make him eat whatever he could. You gotta eat to live.

♪

Right after that, we went on winter break.

When school was off, there was no school lunch. We couldn't let Kosei eat egg sandwiches three meals a day.

I tried really hard to remember his favorite food.

"He likes beef stew, rice omelets, and curry...but who doesn't. Uhhh, besides that, sweet-and-sour pork? That has to have pineapple in it..."

Eating some toast for breakfast at the dining room table, I was muttering to myself and taking notes on the back of a supermarket flyer. Mom started laughing.

"Aren't those all your favorites, Tsubaki?"

"It's okay! I know Kosei eats anything. Anyway, do we have green peppers? I'm gonna make sweet-and-sour pork!"

Wait a minute. Didn't he avoid the pineapple when he had

it at school?

Well, whatever.

I was the one doing the cooking, so I was gonna cook how I liked.

After I finished breakfast, I got right to it. Eyeing the recipe my mom had cut out from a magazine and kept in a scrapbook, I started on the sweet-and-sour pork.

...Sort of.

"Why's it so hard to cut a green pepper? I mean it's slippery and trying to run away from me."

"I'm never cutting onions again ever! I can't see anything from the tears."

"Raw meat feels all flabby when I touch it. Gross."

"Aaagh! I cut my finger!"

"Ack! Smoke's coming outta the oil!"

"Stop, Tsubaki! Are you trying to burn the house down?"

I was gonna put the pork chunks (that I didn't wanna cut into smaller pieces) covered with potato starch (figured out later that I'd used rice flour...) into the fryer, which was giving off a lot of weird smoke. It was really hot, so first I was gonna add some water with a bowl when my mom noticed and, with a frantic look on her face, dashed over and stopped me. She turned the stove off, too.

"What are you doing?! You're gonna get burned badly from the splashing oil! Whew, thank goodness you're all right... Oh, look at your fingers with all those bandages."

Fed up with me, mom let out a big sigh.

"I'm gonna cook for today, Tsubaki, so just help me, okay?"

In the end the only thing I did was to serve it. I wrapped the plate with plastic wrap and put it on a tray to bring it to Kosei's house. It was exactly lunchtime.

"Kosei, here's your lunch. Eat it."

"Thanks. But I don't really have an appetite," he declined with a vague, put-upon smile.

"No, you gotta eat. There's no school lunch. You're gonna get hungry and pass out."

I thrust the tray at him, but he pushed it back. "I'm okay, I have my egg sandwiches. I can eat those."

"You gotta eat other things, you know. I cooked this! So eat it." I wanted him to take it so badly that I lied. "You're saying you can't eat food that I cooked?"

"N-No, I never said that."

We ended up kind of arguing, but he still wouldn't take the tray, and I wondered if the idea of having it alone was making him sad. "Okay, then let's eat together. Don't say no to me. I'm having lunch with you, at your house!"

The school lunch—he does go for that when everyone around him starts digging in.

"Sure," he nodded.

I thought he was on board, but he took the tray from me and retreated into the doorway.

"I'll have it with my dad for dinner. I think he'll be home early today. Thanks."

"Oh, uh, yeah," I said, blinking my eyes, and the door shut.

Should I leave it at that?

The next day, early in the morning, the intercom in our entrance rang.

"Good morning. It's Takahiko from next door."

I opened the door and saw Kosei's dad standing there, dressed casually. He was holding our tray, and on it was the plate for the sweet-and-sour pork, washed clean.

"Good morning," I answered.

"Morning, Tsubaki. I heard you're the one who made this. Great job, it was really tasty. Thank you so much."

Mr. Arima sounded like he felt bad. I felt bad too 'cause it was really my mom who'd made it.

"You're welcome... So it was to your taste?"

"It was really nice of you to make enough for both of us. Kosei told me he had his portion for lunch."

"Uh..."

I'd meant for Kosei to have it to make up for his school lunch. No way had there been enough for two people.

Kosei didn't have any, did he?

As I took the tray, I was so mad.

I'm so gonna make him eat my food—one look and his mouth is gonna water!

That's when my struggles began.

While my mom was at her part-time job, I'd cook all by myself to bring Kosei lunch.

My goal—to make Kosei enjoy my food and make him smile like he used to.

First I tried rice balls...which ended up a mess. How come when I balled the rice it squished out between my fingers and stuck all over my hands?

Then I tried vegetable stir-fry...and burnt it to a crisp.

I tried hamburger steak...which came out raw on the inside and charred on the outside. I thought that was weird, and when I cooked it some more, it exploded. Like with the rice balls, using my hands to bunch the ground meat grossed me out, so I'd put it all in the frying pan as one big piece. I'd figured I could cut it up while it was cooking.

Next up was deep-fried chicken... It came out all raw, too. Hmm, the meat is supposed to be covered in some kind of batter, and you flavor it before you cook it??

Miso soup... It was a little thin so I added some salt, but oops, that was sugar. I couldn't believe how it tasted. Plus, the hefty helpings of *daikon* weren't cooked—maybe I'd cut them too big. The *komatsuna* wasn't sliced through, so the leaves were still linked.

Next I made an omelet...burnt black, again.

"Yuck...even I can't eat my food."

I nibbled on my charred omelet and was put off by how hard and bitter it was.

"There's no way I can give this to Kosei."

Maybe I should quit?

The thought of giving up crossed my mind.

But then I remembered how Kosei had worn a blanket over his head in a pitch-black room, and it just broke my heart.

Am I doing this to make myself feel better?

No.

Not true, I told myself.

The next day would be New Year's Eve, and I still hadn't gotten any better at cooking.

In the morning, I was on my way to the supermarket, thinking hard about what dish I should work at next, when I saw Kosei going into a convenience store.

"Found him!"

Deciding to ask point-blank what he wanted to eat, since I was at a dead end, I followed him inside.

"Kosei!"

"Tsubaki? Thanks for the food the other day. Dad was so happy about it."

He had that same old gentle smile...the one that made it hard to tell what he was actually thinking.

"I cooked it for *you*, okay?!"

"I had some. You added pineapple 'cause that's how you like it, right?"

I knew he was a "no pineapple" person. I'm definitely for it, and I'd gone to the trouble of hiding it under the pork. I guess he'd checked the dish out at least that much.

"Thanks for the comment!"

You didn't actually have to eat any of it to notice.

I grabbed Kosei's collar and wringed his neck, and he flailed his arms and legs.

"But I did have some! And I thought, *She got me.* 'Cause I ate a bit of pineapple by mistake."

"Is—that—true?"

I glared at him. Kosei was so honest that he turned his eyes away.

"Uh...probably."

"What do you mean, probably?"

I flung him away.

I'll cook something he'd wanna eat. I'm not gonna give up until he tries my cooking!

My heart was still pounding as Kosei got closer to the refrigerated section where they had sandwiches and rice balls. He reached for an egg sandwich right in front of me.

"Argh! That, again? Oh wait...you always get it at the bakery, don't you?"

I was talking about the one in the shopping arcade. It's small, but they have tasty stuff.

"Yeah, but it's closed from today till the third."

"Okay, then why don't you choose a different one? Seriously, what do you wanna eat? I'll do my best."

"I'm fine. It must be a lot of trouble. All the effort, and the money, too."

He said it so casually that I got super-mad.

"Trouble?! It's way easier than worrying about you being in a cold, dark house all alone. And money's no problem—I got my New Year's gift allowance in advance. I wanna do it, so it's nothing you need to worry about!"

"Thanks, Tsubaki. I need to pay you back someday."

He smiled and walked toward the cashier like none of this had happened. Next to the register, there was a big pot filled with *oden* stew simmering away. The pot's heat-resistant glass lid wasn't fully on, so steam and the aroma of the broth wafted out through the gap.

"Smells good," I muttered without even thinking.

Kosei gazed melancholically at the steam. "I feel like I wanna offer some to my mom."

"She liked *oden*?"

He put down the egg sandwich at the cashier and turned and glanced at me. Behind his glasses, his eyelashes faced down.

"It was about a year ago...I think," he said. "At the end of last year, when my mom got released from the hospital temporarily, your mom gave us some *oden*. She said she'd made too much. Did you know that?"

"Yeah, I remember."

It wasn't because she'd made too much—she'd made extra for his mom. I'd helped peel the eggs and cut the radish into big chunks (mom peeled it) and tied the seaweed into knots.

Opening his wallet and looking for some coins, Kosei went on wistfully.

"Mom looked so happy when she was eating. At the hospital,

she couldn't have anything that's so hot you have to blow on it. She tried different ingredients little by little... I guess they're called ingredients, right? The different things in *oden*, like radish, fried fish balls, and flat fish cakes? She ate a bit of each, laughing and saying she had such bad manners. I ate what she left."

I got choked up imagining it, and all I could do was nod.

"She said, 'A good neighbor is better than a faraway relative.' She really appreciated it. Thanks for that, Tsubaki."

He'd already finished paying for the egg sandwich.

"I got it!" I grabbed his right wrist. "I'm gonna make *oden*. Kosei, you can choose what I put in it, okay?"

I tugged him all the way out of the convenience store.

"W-Wait, Tsubaki, I didn't even get my egg sandwich!"

"Who cares?"

"I do!"

I made him choose all of the ingredients at the pasted products section in a supermarket. He was surprised to see there were so many kinds to choose from.

For the simmering broth, mom volunteered to supervise because she didn't want the kitchen messed up. She did also check the taste.

It was okay to cut the radish big for this. The same went for the other ingredients. Maybe it was the perfect dish for me to cook.

"Okay, Tsubaki, now you have to watch so it doesn't get burned, and just let it simmer on the lowest heat. It's because you try to hurry and make the fire too strong that it ends up raw inside and charred outside. Just be patient."

I let it simmer all day long like I was told, checking the radish to see if it was cooked, and on the morning of New Year's Eve,

I brought the whole pot over to Kosei. Then mom made some *osechi* New Year's dishes, which I arranged in double boxes and delivered in the evening.

The Arimas were in mourning, so there were no New Year's decorations hanging on the door. Still, Kosei's dad looked so happy about the *osechi*.

Fast forward to the evening of New Year's Day.

The three of us had just come back from our shrine visit. At the entrance, the *oden* pot I'd brought to Kosei was sitting in front of the door, with the lid on tight.

When I lifted it, it was heavier than I expected.

"They didn't eat it?"

I went in and got the lid off in a hurry. The pot had been washed thoroughly, and inside, there were five shiny red apples.

"Apples?"

"Right," mom said, "Saki told me once that she had a relative who lived up north. They sent her apples that she shared with us a few times. That was a long time ago...when Saki was still fine. It was even before...Ko started playing piano every day."

She took the apples from the pot with a nostalgic look on her face.

At the bottom was a note in Kosei's handwriting.

—It was delicious. I could see how you were in the kitchen the whole time. It was piping hot and tasted just like the one from last year, really good. I gave some to my mom, too. Thank you so much. These apples are from her. They sent us a whole box, but you know, just me and dad and mom can't eat so many all on our own.

He ate it, this time.

—The *chikuwa* was so chewy. I didn't know it could be so fluffy and chewy.

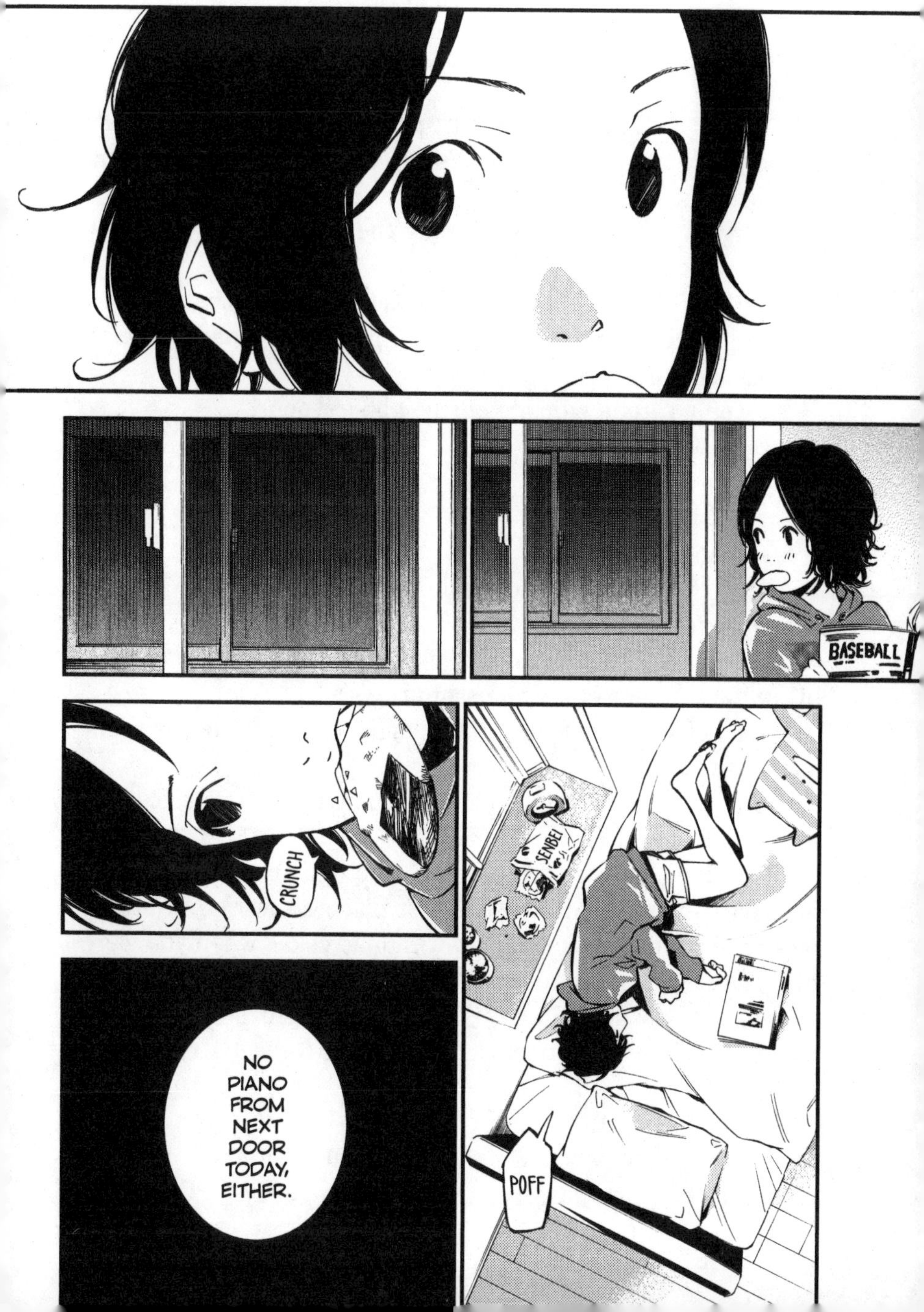
BASEBALL
CRUNCH
SENBEI
POFF
NO PIANO FROM NEXT DOOR TODAY, EITHER.

"That wasn't *chikuwa* but *chikuwabu*. They're totally different. He thought it was *chikuwa* when he picked it out. Oh, Kosei."

Laughing, I quietly wiped away the tears falling down my cheeks with my fingertips.

"I'll go tell Kosei that we can make apple pie before they go bad if they have more," I said to my mom, opened the door, and dashed out.

It's only fifteen steps to our neighbors' door.

♪

A few months later.

Now we were in middle school, where we had to wear a blazer uniform.

From behind, Kosei looked one size bigger as he walked in his uniform under cherry blossom trees.

Still no piano from the Arima residence. It was just as silent as before.

But sometimes, simple melodies came from the music room after class. Gentle notes, played by Kosei.

I decided to join the softball club. At an away match, I learned from an older student that placing the rice in plastic wrap and rolling it, like you did with mud cakes when you were little, was a good way to make rice balls come out fine.

Out in the schoolyard, drinking water to stay hydrated during breaks in practice, I could hear it when I strained my ears.

Kosei playing the piano.

Unlike before, when he played classical music and constantly repeated the same phrases, it was always trendy J-POP with a light touch.

But it only happened once in a while, really...

So I suppose Kosei couldn't totally forget about it.

Even after a somewhat halting piano sounded from the music room after school, the one at his home remained silent. Since that never changed, I figured that was where he was.

How many more years would he be like this, up in the air and lost? Would the Arimas' piano never get played again?

I was unsure for over two years—until the first day of school in April, at the beginning of our third year, at the assembly when my classmate Kaori Miyazono suddenly said something...

♯ 4 ⟦ ♪ Kosei's a Guy ⟧ Ryota Watari

The beginning of this summer, my third year of middle school—
that's when I failed to become a star.

Here's how it was supposed to happen. First the Sumiya
Public Middle School soccer team would win the district
competition, then the city competition, and then the national
competition. And since I'm team captain I get recruited as a J1
youth player or to a high school that has a famous soccer team.
I get picked as a U-18 player for Japan. After graduating high
school, I join some J1 team for a while, and next I represent
Japan in the Olympics, and then do it again in the World Cup.
Then I transfer to a soccer team in England... I have romances
with lots of models, I appear a lot on TV, my memoir becomes a
bestseller, and I'm hounded for autographs everywhere I go—
airports, training locations, you name it.

I, Ryota Watari, who was meant to be a star, lost just like
that in the third round of the district competition, on my home

ground. We lost by one goal.

Now my club activities are done, and I'm still all set to enter some high school with a strong soccer team on a sports recommendation. Meanwhile, all my guy and girl friends are busy going to cram schools or taking practice tests to get into high school, so nobody hangs out with me. Summer's gonna be here for real pretty soon and I'm not gonna have anything to do.

It's a night in July—summer break's starting next weekend.

My sister, a college freshman, stops me in the living room when I come out of the shower.

"Ryota, I've got a present for you. You're gonna love it."

She's been so stingy since she was little. If we had only one piece of cake, she cut it precisely in half, and when there were strawberries on top, she stole one from mine.

Now she's smiling at me in a weird way and holding out some paper ticket holder.

My instincts tell me to be cautious, and I take a step back and hit her with a question.

"You're not gonna charge me for this, are you?"

"Don't worry, it's free, totally free. What's to lose?"

Her fake smile makes me a little suspicious, but I take the ticket holder, which she's thrust into my hand, and ask her another question.

"Are these for food stalls at a summer festival? There's ten of them here."

"Yep, a summer festival on our campus this weekend co-hosted by students and the local shopping arcade. You can use those to buy the most de-li-cious crepes at the stall that my club's running. Use them all up and you get two crepes for free."

"Free crepes? No kidding?"

I get excited for a second. But then my sister is grinning.

"Ah, read closely. 'This ticket can be redeemed for 50 yen off a 250-yen crepe.' So basically, it's a discount ticket."

H-Hey, wait a minute...

"You call that free?!"

"What? Don't complain and just take them!" My sister's eyes look serious...ever since I was little, I've never quarreled with her and won.

"I didn't say I would—"

"If we can't sell them all, it'll be a total wash! Didn't mom teach you not to waste food? Come on, Ryota, come to our festival all three days and buy ten of our crepes! Just do it!!"

"You mean I gotta pay for ten crepes myself? Are you for real? Ten crepes in three days...hang on, weekdays are out, so only Saturday and Sunday? I can't eat all that sweet stuff."

"You're a popular guy. Just bring a different girl each time and you won't even need to eat half of them. Buy them for the girls. There, Ryota," declares my sister, with her hands on her hips and her chest puffed out.

"Say whaaat? You're nuts!"

I protest, but my sister ignores me and escapes into her room.

So that's how this Saturday and Sunday, I've ended up having to invite out one girl I'm friends with after another to ride the trains with me to my sister's college—half an hour with the transfers—to buy them crepes.

Then again, I've been pretty bored lately, so I'm okay with going out on dates. No complaints there.

I have to beg my mom to help me out with some cash, but

even from the station closest to my house, it's half an hour each way, so going-round trip would cost a lot of time and money. My thinking is, every few hours I'll just ask the next girl to come out and meet me at the station near the college campus, and that'll give me some hope of making it through this crazy mission.

"First I'll ask Keiko...then Leina, and after that maybe Mayu?"

Since it's me asking them, they're all more than happy to make time in between cram school sessions to come out.

Finally I'm down to my last two tickets.

"I just gotta use these with Micchan and that'll be it...but all that sweet stuff's got me feeling queasy, I can't eat any more... I'll just give 'em both to her."

So, I message her on LINE.

But this is the answer I get back: "Sorry...but Momo's sick."

"Who?"

"A family member."

"Your little sister?"

"My toy pooh."

????? ...Oh, her toy poodle. Her dog.

"Hope she gets better. Take care of her."

Awww, man. I stare at the two tickets in my hand.

"Who else can I call?"

At the meeting spot in the concourse at the station, lots of people pass me by. Many of them look like groups of students who've gotta be going to my sister's campus.

The ones with the long, thin bags are probably the archery club. And those guys do *kendo*, and those girls must be with the *naginata* club... Oh, they even have lacrosse.

And the group carefully lugging black cases of all different sizes—that must be the orchestra. There's a contrabass, and a cello, and a flute, and a clarinet...

"Ah!"

I've forgotten about picking another girl.

Well, not really, I know who I can call, but she seems pretty busy. I'm sure she's practicing today too.

Kaori Miyazono. She's a violinist. Same class as Tsubaki Sawabe. And really cute.

I get in touch with her.

"Hey, can you come out?"

"Yeah, I just finished practice in the music room, so I'm free."

Practice in the music room...that's Kosei Arima's nest. The kid practically lives there.

At our middle school, the only music club we have is the brass band, and there are so many members that the activities take place in the small gymnasium.

The music teacher spends a ton of time with the brass band, so every afternoon after class and on the weekends, the music room is totally empty. No one uses the piano there.

It's perfect for Kosei Arima, so he's always hanging around there himself. 'Cause it's got a piano. He's gotta have one at home too, but apparently he hasn't been playing that one. Tsubaki lives next door to him and that's what she says, so it must be true.

Kaori's a violinist, so she chose Kosei to be her piano accompanist. I'm not sure but they might have won some competition. Anyway, they were chosen to play in something called a gala concert that's happening at the end of next month.

She explained a little about music competitions once, but

it's all Greek to me. All I know is, I shouldn't cheer Kaori on out loud like at idol group concerts, 'cause at the prelim event the other day I got hushed by Kosei in the audience seats when she was on stage.

Since the beginning of the month, Kaori and Kosei have been practicing in the music room for the gala concert whenever they have time.

I think the song is called Love something-or-other, but I don't really know the title. It's like, dun, da, da, dun, da, da.

When Kaori's playing violin, she's sparkling and super-cute. So, I don't really care about the title. Any song she plays is gonna be beautiful, and poignant, and it'll seep into your heart.

♪

After I wait for Kaori, she runs toward me waving her hand from the station ticket gate. She's carrying a pink violin case and wearing her white shirt and pleated skirt, her summertime school uniform. Even over the weekend, we have to be in uniform if we're gonna be on the school premises.

"Did you come straight from practice?"

"Yeah, I thought I should hurry 'cause today's the last day, right?"

"That's okay, there're so many food stalls competing, so I'm sure there's some left. They're probably starting their bargain sales around now."

"Right! Let's go, let's go. Thanks a lot for inviting me, Ryota."

She gives me a big smile and starts walking almost like she's bouncing along.

If she was gonna be this happy, I should have asked her

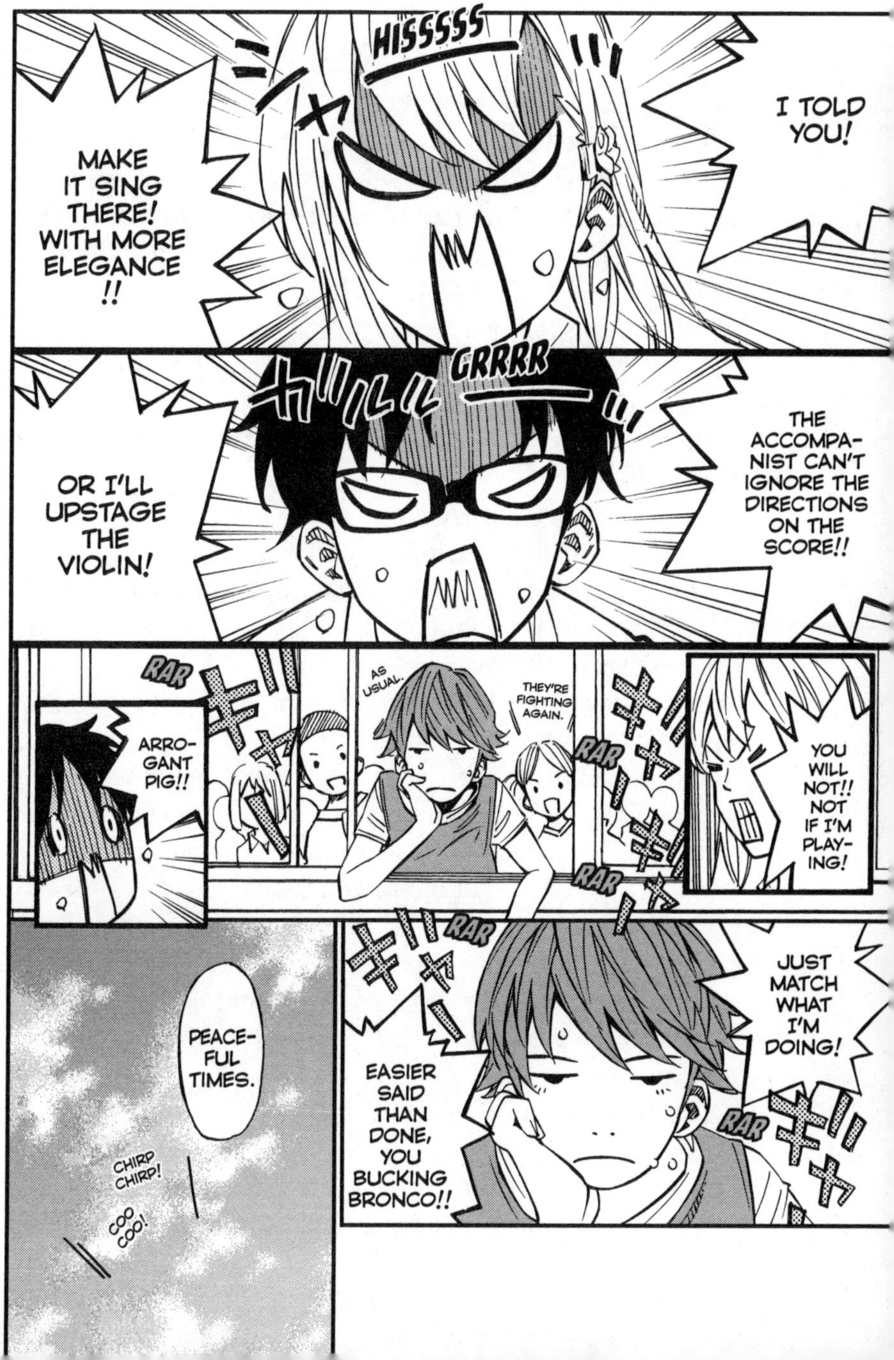
HISSSSS
I TOLD YOU!
MAKE IT SING THERE! WITH MORE ELEGANCE!!
GRRRR
THE ACCOMPANIST CAN'T IGNORE THE DIRECTIONS ON THE SCORE!!
OR I'LL UPSTAGE THE VIOLIN!
YOU WILL NOT!! NOT IF I'M PLAYING!
RAR
RAR
THEY'RE FIGHTING AGAIN.
AS USUAL.
RAR
ARROGANT PIG!!
JUST MATCH WHAT I'M DOING!
RAR
RAR
EASIER SAID THAN DONE, YOU BUCKING BRONCO!!
PEACEFUL TIMES.
CHIRP CHIRP!
COO COO!

from the beginning.

I thought she'd be with Kosei...

"I love crepes! Especially with strawberry and whipped cream in it." She's glowing and looks really excited. "Nothing tastes as good as crepes, y'know? Whoever came up with them should be thanked by the whole world!"

"Hahaha...isn't that a little much?"

"No, it's so-o-o true...but I like waffles, too. And mille-feuille, and tiramisu, and trifles! Ahh, I can't choose!"

Yeah, I think that means she likes almost all fancy sweets. But whatever.

We pass through the entrance of the college, which looks really gaudy from all the balloon decorations they've put up.

Inside, it's a jumble, with voices announcing last calls, people hurrying to get home, and others rushing in, relieved that the festival's still on.

I've got the route down pat by now and make my way through the sea of bodies.

"Kaori, the stall for my sister's club is between the second and third building—huh? Where'd she go?" I thought she was following me, but now she's nowhere to be found. "I lost her? Guess she's the type to get distracted easily."

I start looking for her and find her following a crowd walking toward the gate. She has a small digital camera in her hand.

"Excuse me, Miss. You dropped this camera! Miiiiss!"

The lady she's calling "Miss" looks over fifty—from any angle.

"Oh, thank you so much, young lady."

"You're welcome."

I figure that's what they're saying to each other, but I can't make it across the waves of people to get to her. The best I can do is to keep her in sight through the gaps so I don't lose her.

After saying goodbye and waving to the woman, who's bowing again and again, Kaori turns this way.

"Hey, Kaori! Over here."

"Ah, Ryota."

As she's trying to cross through the crowd, her head sinks and I lose her again.

"Geez, did she fall?"

In a panic, I desperately cut through, going, *Excuse me, let me through, please, excuse me...*

And there's Kaori, crouching and holding a little girl who's around five years old.

"You fell down. It doesn't hurt? Are you okay?"

The girl nods. "You caught me, so I'm okay."

"Good, I'm glad I made it." Kaori flashes an easygoing smile. "Do you know where your parents are?"

"Yup, over there." There's a woman who's talking to another woman under some trees. "She said I could buy *takoyaki*."

"By yourself? That's not a good idea. I'll go with you, and he will too."

Kaori points at me as I just stand there.

"Uhh..." the little girl answers, looking at me like following a strange guy isn't what she's been taught to do.

"Okay," I say, "I'll go get it. Kaori, stay with her where her mom can see you."

Kaori smiles. "Thanks, Ryota. You're such a decent guy."

"Here," the girl sticks out her right hand.

"You can give me the money later in exchange," I tell her. "Just one pack, right?"

"Yeah! But no seaweed flakes."

"All right."

I buy a pack of *takoyaki* from the nearest stall and give it to the girl. She gives me the money, and I finally start walking side by side with Kaori again.

But...

"Meow," Kaori suddenly makes this weird sound.

"Huh?"

"Meow! Cats, cats, look at all the kitties!"

"Yeah, my sis told me there're lots of stray cats living on campus."

"Meoww!"

There are stalls everywhere, not only on the asphalt streets but on the grassy courtyard between the buildings.

With the hem of her skirt waving, Kaori runs off behind a tent after two cats. One of them is black-and-white, and the other one's a tiger color.

I yell, "W-Wait, it's not safe back there!" Gas cylinders, motors that run on oil, electric cables, and all kinds of stuff are lying around. "Phew, can't take your eyes off of her... In more ways than one."

The other girls stayed close to me, happily gazing up at my face in this flirty way. When our eyes met, they'd look down all of a sudden, kind of blushing.

But Kaori is attracted to so many things. She said she was my fan...before running into a concert hall to play violin, choosing Kosei as her piano accompanist, drawing me and Tsubaki in, and then practicing alone with Kosei.

"Kaori!"

I search for her and find her behind a bench that's falling apart. She's making a shadow with her body for the two cats as they eat some chicken on the grass. Maybe they'd gotten it from someone.

"The sun's come out. It's hot, isn't it? Maybe the rainy season's gonna be over soon."

My shadow and Kaori's are visible on the green grass, but right away the sun gets covered up and they disappear.

Kaori looks up at the sky. I do the same, too. I see these dull-colored clouds floating by quickly.

"It's still so cloudy..." Kaori shades her eyes with her hand, squinting. The cats finish eating the chicken and run off somewhere. "Aw, the kitties are gone," she says. "They were so fluffy, I wanted to pet them."

"There are plenty of cats here. Hey, we better hurry and get some crepes... They might get sold out, after all."

"Oh right!"

We head for the crepe stall...or we try to, anyway.

When we get closer to a square surrounded by school buildings, we start to hear music.

It's the orchestra club I saw before.

"Come on over and show off your musical skills. Who wants to try?"

"Play against us one on one—get more applause than we do and win one of these prizes!"

There's this low, makeshift stage made of beer cases and plywood surrounded by a crowd of people, like a live street show. On top are several people holding acoustic stringed and wind instruments. What they're giving away is stuff like mini-towels and notepads and other original merchandise from the university that have the school colors.

"I want that!"

Kaori's got her eyes on this little figurine with a strap that you can use as an earphone jack.

"What, that iffy thing? It's the school mascot... They sell

that at the co-op."

"But it means more if you win it!" No sooner than she says this, Kaori takes her pink violin case off her back. "Me! Me! I wanna try!"

She pushes her way through the crowd and goes to the stage. I rush after her, making for the front of the ring of spectators.

The pleats of Kaori's skirt are fluttering as she hops on stage, and with her left hand she grabs her violin by the neck... or whatever it's called...the thin tip part, and holds it up high. In her right hand, she's got her stick—I think maybe it's called a bow, the thing you play with.

Then a guy student who's hosting the show says in a high-pitched voice, "Ohh, she's got her own instrument! Looks like we've got a tough opponent here! Now then, you'll be going up against the head of our club. Miss Furukawa, if you please."

A female student in a dark dress comes out from behind the stage. She's holding a violin and is pretty good-looking.

The first thing she does after getting the mic from the host is to shake hands with Kaori. Then she explains the deal.

"Are you in high school? Or maybe middle school? Since you're the challenger, you get to pick the song. But please understand that you'll be playing unaccompanied. As for sheet music, we do have some with us, but if we don't have it, you'll have to play from memory. We will, too. All right, please go ahead and tell us what you'd like to play."

With the mic pointed at her, Kaori puts on a serious face and answers, "'Love's Joy,' by Fritz Kreisler. I'll be playing from memory."

"That's quite a famous piece. Why are you going with that?"

"I wanted to play it together with someone, but 'Sorrow'

suits him more now, so I decided to play that one with him. But 'Joy' speaks more to how I feel, so I want to play it on my own."

Kaori's eyes are so full of light when she replies. She's looking out straight ahead.

Love something-or-other...playing it together... Does she mean...

"Yes, 'Love's Joy' and 'Love's Sorrow' form a pair. Both are wonderful pieces, aren't they? Very good, please go ahead and begin."

The young woman in the dress steps back.

Kaori takes two deep breaths and mumbles something to herself. She comes to the middle of the stage and bows. With a serious look, she puts her violin on her left shoulder and gets her stick ready.

The crowd grows quiet, and all attention's on her. Suddenly I hear this annoying buzzing in the background.

It's the hawkers at the stalls, announcements being called out, and dance music, too.

Then Kaori starts playing, and her violin breaks right through all that.

Ta-ta-tum, ta-la-la, ta-la-la-la-lum. Ta-la-la, ta-la-la, ta-la-la...

It's a fun song that sounds kinda like that.

Ah, that's not the song she's practicing with Kosei.

It's got a totally different mood, plus I've heard it somewhere before. It feels like something you'd hear after the toast at a wedding.

She makes her strings sing, and her sounds bounce. She's keeping the rhythm with her whole body, the tip of her ponytail waving around. She looks like she's having fun playing her violin.

The crowd starts getting into it, too. Some people are swaying their bodies a little to the music, some are keeping rhythm by snapping their fingers, and others are closing their eyes and letting the song take them far away.

Kaori's violin carries really well, and it's beautiful. It trickles down to the bottom of my heart. It doesn't go in one ear and out the other. It doesn't just brush over my skin.

I'm the kind of guy who almost never listens to classical music, but she's so good that even I can tell her sound hits you in the pit of your stomach.

Ta-laa-la-la—lum!

The last note of her violin blends into the sky, where a pillar of light has descended from between the clouds.

For a moment the crowd goes silent, like time has stopped, but then after a second they give her a big round of applause. "Erupting" actually seems like the right word.

"Bravo!" one older guy shouts. Some kid is clapping his hands hard with these big gestures.

Kaori's cheeks turn red, and she bows deeply.

The female student with the black dress walks towards her as she claps.

"It's obvious that you're much better than me," she says with an awkward smile, "so I don't think I should play. Thank you so much. You were really amazing."

But Kaori looks a little frustrated.

"You're not going to play? That's not fair. Why don't we all together? You guys, too!" Kaori invites the club members standing in the back and by the stage, instruments in hand, and brings them forward one after another. "Are there any sheets we can play as an ensemble? Let's enjoy this!"

And they start playing a song called "Mozart's whatchamacallit." I think I've heard it somewhere...back in grade school, during announcements to tell us it was time for cleaning duty... Nah, I don't know the title.

After another big round of applause, and an encore, Kaori finally comes back. Even I know the encore song: "Twinkle, Twinkle, Little Star," but with a lot of arrangements.

"Aww, it was so much fun!" Swinging the mascot item she received, she comes back to me. She says, "Life is wonderful, isn't it? So much to enjoy."

Her smiling face is gleaming white and it's almost blinding.

Hm, she suddenly puts her index finger to her chin. "Ryota, what were we doing next?"

"Crepes."

"Right! Crepes! I hope they still have strawberry ones."

"They might run out if we don't hurry, you know?"

"Yikes, let's go!"

"Yeah."

Kaori can't keep up with me because I start running and she can't dodge all these people. Realizing that she's worried about the violin on her back, I offer to hold the case, but she gently refuses my help.

I take her hand.

"Is it okay?"

Her hand is a little cold. I've never touched it before...and the faintest sense of guilt starts bubbling up in me. It ends up a small black stain in my heart.

It feels somehow like Kaori's not a girl that I should touch casually.

♪

With Kaori's hand in mine, the two of us finally make it to the stall run by my sister's club. She's been waiting. She glares at me, and I let Kaori's hand go in a hurry.

"Ryota, you're late. We're about to close up. I kept some for you, so you're welcome." Maybe my sister is kind, after all. She adds, "I was getting nervous. I texted you on LINE a lot but you didn't answer."

Of course not—listening to Kaori's awesome playing was more important.

Showing a fake smile to Kaori, who's on the verge of asking me who the lady might be, my sister drags me aside.

"Hey, this last girl is the cutest. Is she the one?"

"What are you talking about? That's rude to the other girls. They're all cute."

"How like you, Ryota."

My sister shoves me away, and once she goes back to the stall, she puts two crepes on a paper plate—one with strawberries and whipped cream, and the other with canned mixed fruit and whipped cream—with chocolate sauce on top of both, and brings them to me. They're kinda squished a bit, but they look okay considering it's a stall run by amateurs.

"All right, these are all we've got left. No complaints, now."

She takes the two tickets and the four hundred yen I'm holding out and just disappears.

"Whew, I'm glad they still had strawberries..."

I go back to Kaori, who can hardly wait, and we sit down side by side on an open bench nearby.

"It's my treat, so go ahead and eat all you want."

"Strawberries! Yay! Thanks so much, Ryota."

Kaori shovels the crepe into her mouth and has this look of genuine happiness. She scarfs it down in no time.

"You can have mine too."

"Really? Thank you!"

Kaori goes right ahead and takes a bite of the mixed fruit crepe, and then stops.

"Oh, is two too much for you?" I ask, worried.

Kaori shakes her head. "Uh-uh... If I eat it at once, it'll be gone. I wanna savor and enjoy it."

"Oh, okay."

Kaori gazes at the pillar of light that's stretching down from the bluish-gray clouds. "See that? That's what they call an angel's ladder. Whenever you see one, an angel is coming down from heaven to guide a soul... It's so beautiful, it's sad, isn't it?"

"Huhh?"

Kaori never gazes at me or anything. I mean like other girls do, romantically—or even look down bashfully.

She has something totally different in sight.

She's so unlike those other girls who're interested in me.

But...she does look at Kosei Arima. She makes eye contact with him and sometimes even stares at him. I've noticed that much. From way back.

...Since the beginning.

"Hey, Kaori. What's the name of that song you played? It's also called 'Love Something-or-Other,' right?"

"I wanted to play it together with someone."

That someone has to be Kosei.

Kaori nods yes. She's still looking far off when she answers, "'Love's Joy.' It's paired with the song we're practicing and is by the same composer. The one we're practicing is 'Love's Sorrow.'"

"Huh. Yeah, I guess the one you play with Kosei does sound a little sad...the one today felt more cheerful."

"Kreisler, who composed it about a hundred years ago, didn't tell people at first that it was his own work. He wasn't just a composer but a very popular performer. It's said that he put the audience in a happy mood just by going on stage, before he even played. He wrote short pieces running about three and half minutes like 'Love's Joy' and 'Love's Sorrow' to play for encores but told people, 'I happened to find some old sheets of music in a library in Vienna. It's probably dance music from the past, and young couples must have danced to it and fallen in love.'

"Works with some kind of backstory tend to please people more. You know, like Beethoven's 'Destiny' or 'Pastoral,' instead of opus numbers with just letters and numerals in them. Nicknames give you a certain image, and anecdotes help people remember. 'It was dedicated to a girl he had a crush on, but she was from a noble family so it didn't work out,' or something like that."

Kaori says all this without pausing. Like she's been wanting to tell someone.

"But twenty or so years later, this newspaper reporter did some digging and got the scoop that there were no such songs in Vienna and that Kreisler made it all up. That made Kreisler really angry, which was apparently rare for him. I think he wanted to say, 'What's the harm in coming up with a story that people can dream about and enjoy?' Going so far as to lie... to tell a beautiful lie so people can dream...that's what artists, entertainers, do."

"I think I get your point, somehow."

We need dreams that are prettier than reality in order to live—right?

"So, Kaori, you decided to play a song that comes with a

dream with Kosei."

"Because I found it." She smiles to herself, looking a teeny bit sad, but also proud.

"Where?"

"Didn't you hear from Tsubaki? One day we were all wet and I dropped by his house 'cause he said I could dry off my clothes there. Anyway, there's this dusty piano, and on top of it are the sheet music for 'Love's Sorrow' and 'Love's Joy,' both of them, also covered in dust. But 'Love's Sorrow' looked like it'd been used a lot more. For some reason."

"I guess Kosei likes the song?"

Kaori shakes her head. "I'm not sure. But I want him to play it... Not 'Joy,' which I like better, but 'Sorrow,' which he knows. Any way he interprets it is fine with me, I can follow the tune."

I thought Kosei once said the piano accompaniment's task is to faithfully follow the violin as it plays freely?

"Kaori, you like Kosei...'s music, don't you."

My hearts starts to ache a little. I couldn't ask her if she likes Kosei himself.

"Yeah, I do. I really like all of you, a lot. I'm so glad that I'm alive and that there are so many things that I love. Being able to play the violin, people listening to my performances and applauding, and crepes, too."

Kaori takes another bite and then looks up at the sky and spreads her arms. Her eyes are wavering. They're sparkling, but also wavering somehow...

"I love every day. I love everything."

I get the feeling that I'm nothing special to her. Maybe I'm part of her "everything," but I'm not special compared to everything else.

Yeah, of course. I don't treat Kaori differently from other girls, either.

But Kosei...he must be special to Kaori.

From the beginning, Kaori was always taking Kosei by the hand. Like when they went to the concert hall under an April blizzard of cherry blossom petals. She was looking straight at him.

Unlike Kosei, I can't play piano. I don't know a thing about classical music. The only topics that Kaori and I have in common are Kosei and Tsubaki.

He can give her tons more joy and happiness than I can. If she keeps on smiling happily, I'm good.

I want to see her smiling, eating sweets, and laughing, chasing after cats. I want to see her feeling good making beautiful music with her violin, forever.

"Kaori, I guess practicing with Kosei also makes you happy?"

"Yep." She finally looks straight at me and gives a big nod.

"You know...Kosei's a guy."

"Huh? I know."

"Well, as long as you do."

What she means by "know" is a whole other question.

He lost his mom when he was in sixth grade, and up to the end of the second year of middle school, he was an empty husk.

But after meeting Kaori in April, at the beginning of our third year, he came alive again.

Always thinking of her, he follows along and humors her even when she's a handful.

He's...a guy. A guy who can treasure one girl. He's become a real guy.

I wonder if I should tell her what I mean by "guy"...and

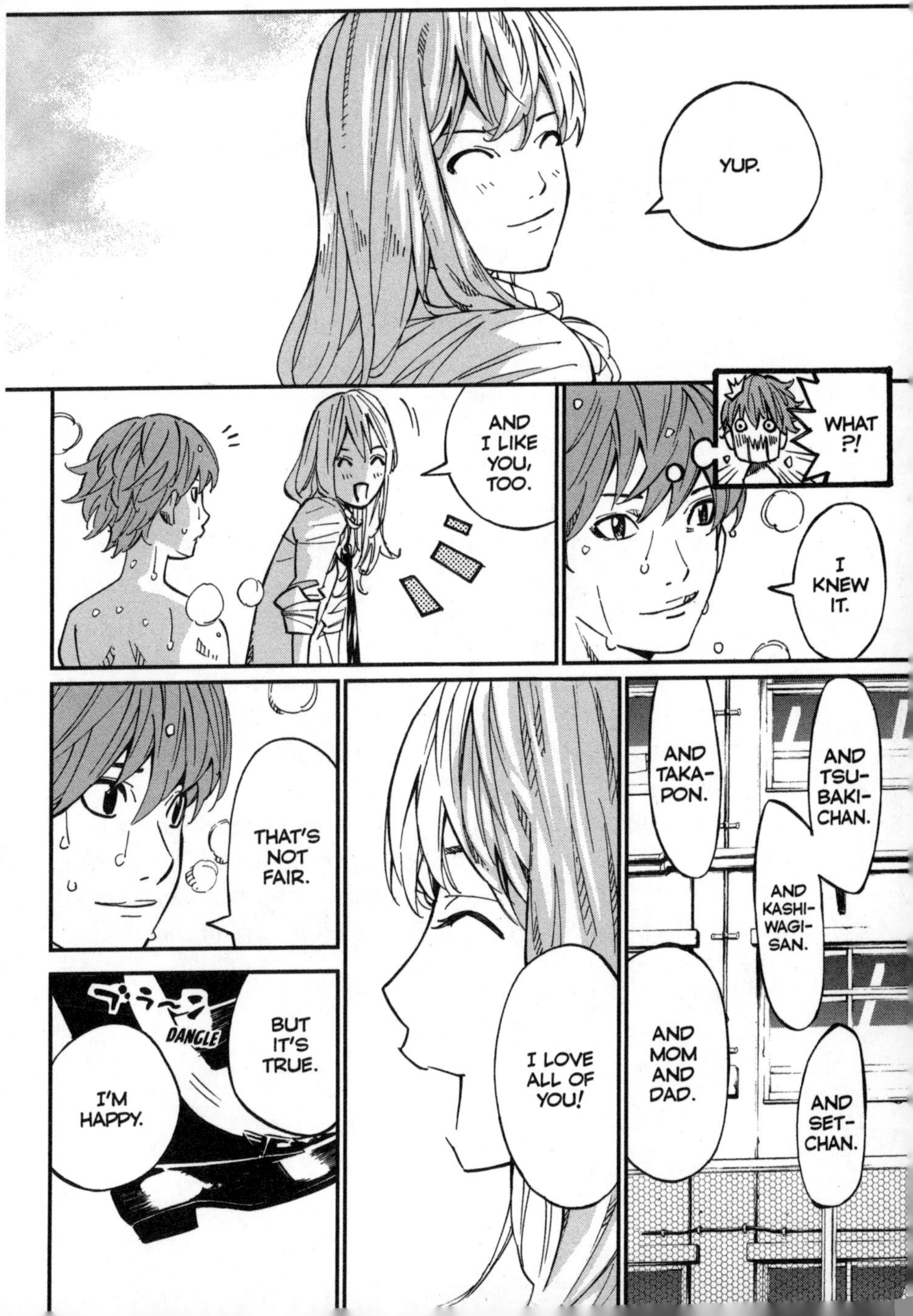

YUP.
AND I LIKE YOU, TOO.
WHAT?!
I KNEW IT.
THAT'S NOT FAIR.
BUT IT'S TRUE.
DANGLE
I'M HAPPY.
I LOVE ALL OF YOU!
AND TAKAPON.
AND TSUBAKI-CHAN.
AND KASHIWAGI-SAN.
AND MOM AND DAD.
AND SET-CHAN.

drop it.

It's something Kosei should tell her. When he thinks he has to, and in his own words.

Kaori doesn't need to know until then.

"I think it's great that you and Kosei have gotten so close, you know."

I mean it when I say it, and Kaori turns to me with this beautiful smile on her face. She's got some whipped cream from the crepe on her cheek.

Then the clouds break, and these faint beams pour down on her. The fringes of her light-colored hair begin to sparkle, and it makes such an impression on me.

"Thanks, Ryota. Hearing you say that...is a relief. Thanks so much."

That moment. She looks unforgettably beautiful.

"You're the best!" she tells me.

Suddenly, she tears off half of the crepe she's eating and shoves it into my mouth.

Ugh, that's sweet. Sis must've dumped all the chocolate sauce she had left.

Kaori's laughing so hard at the look on my face. The sound of her voice, the pillar of white light, the violin music that she played alone, the sweetness of chocolate and whipped cream mixed with a bit of bitterness, all these things are branded deep in my heart—

I still haven't forgotten.

Epilogue 〖 ♪ You're Amazing 〗 Kaori Miyazono

Here in the music room, only you and I are left.

"Okay, let's start again! Get the tempo of your piano right this time. First, dum, da, da, dum, da, da. From the *poco ritardando* [gradually slowing down a bit], it's duum, dah, dah. Slow it down like so, and then do the *tempo primo* [going back to the original speed], where you repeat that first dum, da, da."

I tap the edge of the music stand.

"Yup, sure," you mutter, seated on the piano chair, "if you keep that tempo for your violin, that'll fix the problem."

"Ack... I do more or less, don't I?"

You reply calmly. "It can't be 'more or less' for my piano to match well, you know? I keep the tempo precisely according to the length of the key on the sheet."

"What, are you saying I have a bad sense of rhythm? Fine." I go over to the CD player on the teacher's desk. "Let's dance and see which one of us has a worse sense of rhythm. You're

153

precise like a metronome, but you don't pay enough attention to details like subtle shifts. That big head of yours is all full of logic—you don't feel the rhythm with your whole body, do you?"

I pick up from beside the player the CD that I brought. I haven't listened to it yet, so I'm really excited.

"What CD is that?"

"It's 'Love's Sorrow.' The violin's played by the composer Fritz Kreisler himself."

Your eyes open wide with surprise. You ask, "I knew he was a performer, but you can get an audio recording? Of course, since he was active in the twentieth century, after Edison, there must have been recording devices... Is that a remaster of the original record or something?"

"Yup. There are CDs for recordings from like a hundred years ago, but this one's newer, recorded in 1938. And—it cost just two hundred yen at the big supermarket in front of the station three stops ahead of ours. I found it in the bargain bin!"

I walk towards you and hold out the CD case so you can get a closer look at the price tag. It's on the plastic wrap. Then I tear off the wrapping.

"It was on sale 'cause no one wanted it? Feels even cheaper," you say with a wry smile.

"Whatever. Forget people who don't appreciate its value. For us, it's an almost divine performance. If the composer's directions on the sheet are absolute, like you say, then let's find out if he followed his own directions when he played it."

I pop the CD in the player, press the button, and choose "Love's Sorrow."

Amidst a bit of noise and kind of missing the echo, violin music starts flowing.

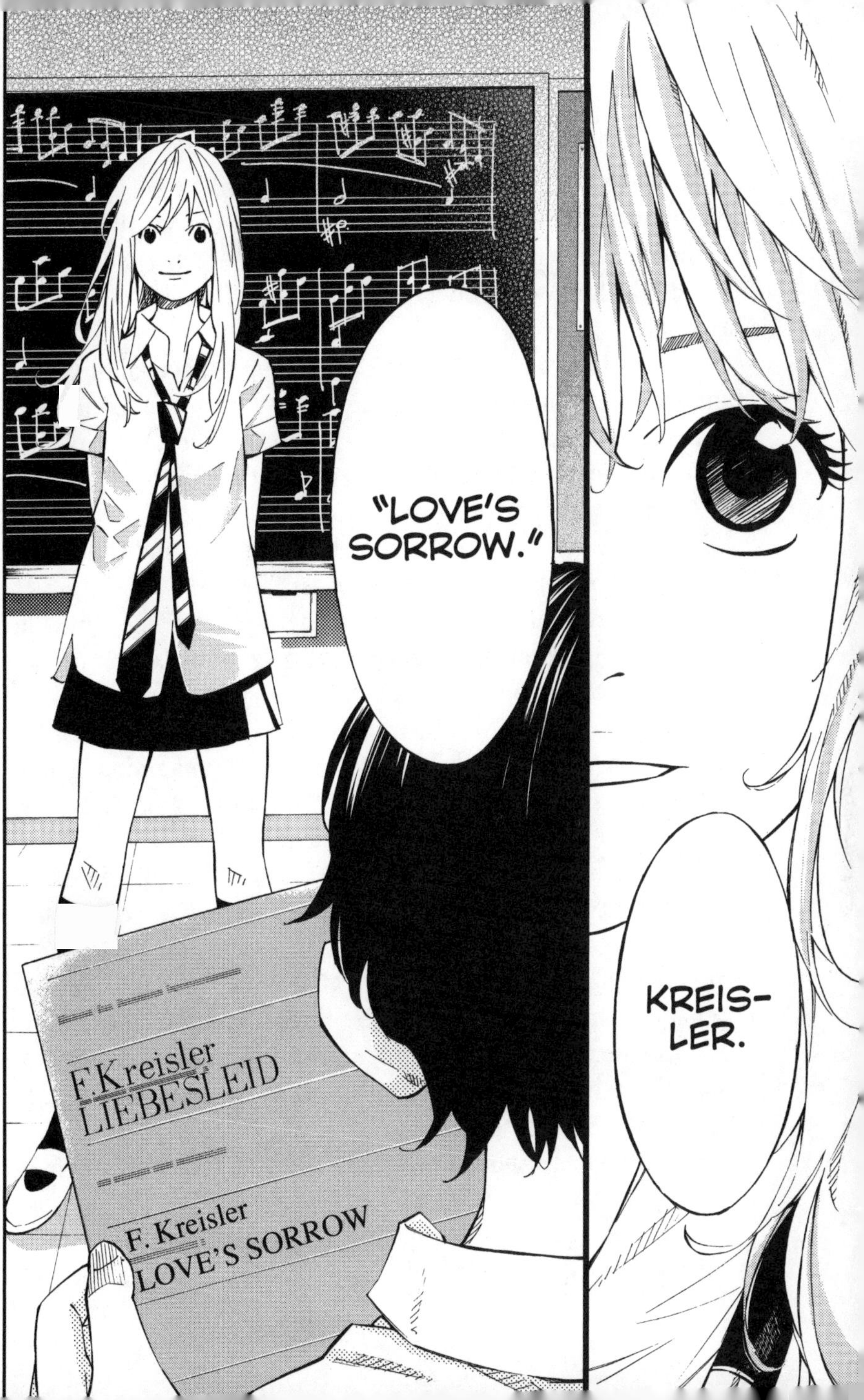
KREIS-
LER.
"LOVE'S
SORROW."
F.Kreisler
LIEBESLEID
F. Kreisler
LOVE'S SORROW

"Now, let's dance. Let's see about your famous tempo directed by the sheet. We'll try to feel it with our whole bodies."

I hold out my hand, but you softly, gently reject me.

"I don't think we need to dance. We can figure it out just by listening."

"This song was created as dance music, according to the composer's own story. Just 'cause we've never danced a waltz in a castle in Vienna doesn't mean we can't dance. C'mon!"

But you just smile vaguely and don't stand up.

"Forget it, I'll dance alone. Watch."

I press rewind to get back to the beginning and then start dancing, extending my limbs freely, as I please.

It's a sorrowful melody, and the rhythm's in triple time like a waltz. The little bit of noise adds a nostalgic note.

The directions on the sheet don't tell you how many beats there are in a second or a minute. "Start with the *Ländler* tempo, then *espressivo* [play expressively]; imagining a past love, feelings pour out; slow down *grazioso* [gracefully]. Go back to the original speed. Repeat." That's all it says.

Ländler is an old kind of dance music in triple time that originated in and around Austria. I don't know how fast it is, never having heard a real *Ländler*. I think it must have been leisurely like a folk song. It's said that once the waltz became popular, *Ländler* fell off 'cause the tempo was too slow.

The direction that the composer put on the sheet says to mimic the tempo of an old tradition that vanished a long time ago, that nobody remembers.

So why worry about how many beats a second it ought to be?

Expressively, emotionally, gracefully—all you've gotta do is follow those directions and play at whatever tempo you like.

I pull off two elegant turns on my toes and finish by striking a pose.

You clap for me.

"That was wonderful."

"Thank you."

I bow, and when I look up you're already facing the piano, your long fingers on the keyboard.

"I figured out the tempo," you say. "I go with what the composer himself played at, right?"

You start, and it's the exact same tempo as the CD, an almost punishingly accurate reproduction.

"Your turn—play your violin. At this tempo."

I'm appalled by your direction, but I pick up my violin from the desk.

Overlaying the image that the CD gave me, I caress the strings.

They resonate, and the vibrations seep into my body.

Yes...little by little, your piano and my violin are meshing together.

You're amazing. You've already grasped the tempo that feels best to me.

Your piano feels so good.

That's why I wanna play for all I'm worth, of course.

You're really amazing.

I'm so glad I could perform with you.

Laying my sound over your piano makes me happy. It's so fun. It quickens my pulse.

My heart's pounding. It's almost hard to breathe.

You're amazing. Amazing, all right?

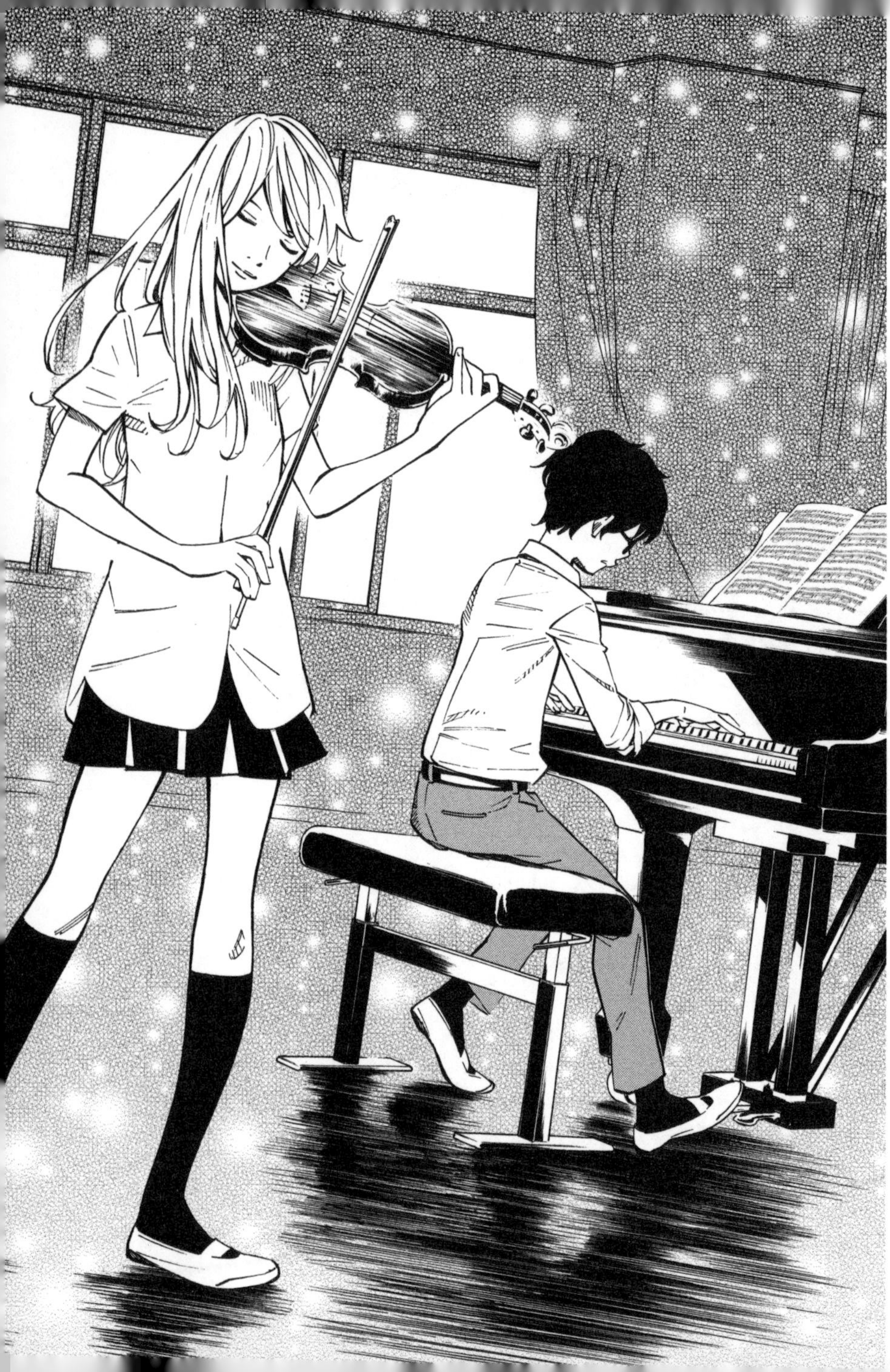

Afterword

I always wanted to write a story someday that makes you feel like you're hearing music.

I'd like to express my appreciation to those who granted me this opportunity to novelize the manga *Your Lie in April*. The original story is very beautiful and poignant and has a certain pain and sweetness and bitterness. I was really drawn to it.

Describing music in words is very challenging. Before I began, the editor-in-chief gave me a serious look and asked me:

"Music, tones—how do you intend to convey all that?"

I remember answering that abstract expressions based on imagery wouldn't be enough and that I wanted to portray in as particular a manner as possible a character who understood music logically via language and numerical values.

I would include scenes that weren't lyrical so that the lyricism would stand out.

Shaking off my anxiety over whether I have something to

show for all my effort, I humbly present this book to you, dear readers.

I assume many of you have some experience learning how to play piano. I, too, took lessons when I was a child.

I'm one of those people who quit, bored with Czerny Exercises, because I needed to study for high school entrance exams. Let alone becoming a concert pro, I wasn't aiming for a career as a pianist.

The only Beethoven that I can play is "Für Elise," the only Mozart is the "Turkish March," so forget Chopin—that's my level.

For a while, I played anime songs and such for fun on weekends, but once I started getting busy with my first job, without even realizing it I stopped opening the lid of my piano.

On this occasion, after a long hiatus, I tried playing the upright piano at my parents' house. Since they play and have it tuned annually, the instrument itself is still in active service.

I opened up the score to Bach's "The Well-Tempered Clavier Book 1: 1," famous as the piano accompaniment to Gounod's "Ave Maria," hoping that I could play something as simple as that on first sight. (The piece makes an appearance in this work.)

If only haltingly, I managed to, which was kind of satisfying. I was surprised that my fingers remembered.

I've written a lot of novelizations about characters facing all sorts of challenges, but most of the time, I lack any personal experience and need to use my imagination based on ongoing research.

This time was different. Perhaps because the little

experience and knowledge that I do have was getting in my way, just tapping my PC keyboard didn't lead to the best expressions. Obtaining and spreading out scores next to me, I had to tap the desk with my fingers. "Air piano" was what I required to proceed.

It was a strange experience for me. I'd been presumptuous enough to think that I could write novels in my head, so it was humbling.

Actually, the CD that Kaori shows off (?) in the epilogue owes to a real-life episode. I'd searched a long time online for a recording and finally procured one, but three days later, just like I wrote in this book, I found one in a bargain bin. At that moment, a certain teacher named Nozomu Itoshiki shouted "I'm in despair!" in my heart (lol).

When I checked, the year was different from the recording I already had, so of course I bought it.

For all of the pieces mentioned in the original manga or to be used in the anime, and also for any that I wanted to include in these stories, I ransacked my house for the CDs I'd collected when I was younger. (Before becoming a novelist, I'd been in a chorus group that often sang classical music, so I was a semi-serious classical fan at the time. For me, competitions meant chorus competitions). The ones I didn't have, I bought, and I listened to all of the songs as I worked. In fact, I'd never written while listening to music before. I felt sort of renewed.

I really loved music. I do even now, deep down. Classical especially.

So I was hoping to one day tell a story that makes you feel like you're hearing music.

But my interest shifted to storytelling itself, and that became my job. It became my whole life, to the point where I didn't listen to music anymore.

Now I'm thinking I'd like to start listening to music again. I hope I can get going with the chorus, too!

Finally, I'd like to express my gratitude to everyone involved.

To Naoshi Arakawa-sensei, to the Monthly Shonen Magazine editorial department, to Miss Etsuko Oguchi, a piano teacher who handled the research and fact-checking, and to the editor in charge, and everyone else who devoted themselves to this publication—thank you so much for your guidance.

Most of all, I thank all of you from the bottom of my heart, dear readers, for picking up these stories.

Yui Tokiumi
while listening to Kreisler's last recorded performance of "Love's Sorrow," from 1942

About the Authors

Before she became a novelist, author **Yui Tokiumi** worked at a museum where she was engaged in archaeological and ethnographic research. She is known for her adaptations of classical Japanese literature as well as of quality comics.

Creator **Naoshi Arakawa** won the 37th Kodansha Manga Award (Boys Division) for *Your Lie in April* only several years after making his debut. His latest offering features high school women's soccer.

Your Lie in April

A LIFE IN MONOTONE

Kosei Arima was a piano prodigy until his mother died suddenly, changing his life forever. Driven by his pain to abandon piano, Kosei now lives in a colorless world. He has resigned himself to a bland life, until he meets Kaori Miyazono—a violinist with an unorthodox style. Can she bring Kosei back to music, and back to life?

A YALSA "Great Graphic Novels for Teens" Selection!

ATTACK ON TITAN: BEFORE THE FALL

The first of the franchise's light novels, this prequel of prequels details the origins of the devices that humanity developed to take on the mysterious Titans.

ATTACK ON TITAN: KUKLO UNBOUND

Swallowed and regurgitated as an infant by a Titan, an orphan seeks to find and prove himself in this official prequel novel to the smash hit comics series.

ATTACK ON TITAN: LOST GIRLS

LOST GIRLS tells of the times and spaces in between the plot points, through the eyes and ears of the saga's toughest—but more taciturn—heroines.

LEARN MORE AT

IN NOVEL FORM!

ATTACK ON TITAN:
THE HARSH MISTRESS
OF THE CITY Part 1

A stand-alone side story, *Harsh Mistress* tells of the increasingly harrowing travails of Rita Iglehaut, a Garrison soldier trapped outside the wall, and her well-to-do childhood friend Mathias Kramer.

ATTACK ON TITAN:
THE HARSH MISTRESS
OF THE CITY Part 2

In this concluding half, Rita Iglehaut struggles to turn her isolated hometown into something of a city of its own. Her draconian methods, however, shock the residents, not least Mathias Kramer, her childhood friend.

ATTACK ON TITAN:
END OF THE WORLD

In this novelization of the theatrical adaptation, the series' familiar setting, plot, and themes are reconfigured into a compact whole that is fully accessible to the uninitiated and strangely clarifying for fans.

THE SEVEN DEADLY SINS

Seven Scars They Left Behind

Princess Margaret and young Gilthunder know the terrible truth about the betrayal but dare not speak of it, not even to each other.

The aftermath of the event that shook Liones comes to life in seven prose side stories illustrated by Suzuki himself.

Stories by Shuka Matsuda
Created by Nakaba Suzuki

AVAILABLE NOW FROM VERTICAL, INC.